THE WORLD BLEEDS

THE WORLD BURNS - BOOK 3

BOYD CRAVEN

The World Bleeds, The World Burns Book 5
By Boyd Craven

Many thanks to friends and family for keeping me writing! Special thanks to Jenn, who's helped me with my covers from day one and keeps me accountable!!!!!

TABLE OF CONTENTS

CHAPTER 1

PINHOTI TRAIL, ALABAMA

I got another one," Bret's voice called down into the cave.

"You know, the kid's getting pretty good at this," John said to Michael.

"He is. I just wish we had more… Do you think it'd be safe for us to see if our houses are still there?" Michael asked.

"Soon. Your turn to dress the rabbit out." John teased.

Michael smiled at John. "Better than stinky fish?"

"Better than stinky fish," John grinned, and they headed out of the cave.

Bret was dancing around the entrance and Linny was all smiles. Both kids had grown accustomed to the 'camping experience'. They were all getting tired of low rations, but since the kids were becoming proficient trappers things, weren't so bad. The information on the radio wasn't always the most optimistic, but it wasn't the same looped crap they had first found.

Groups had sprung up on the radio from all over the country. Sometimes Michael would listen in for hours at a time, rarely speaking. Other times he'd get on there and tentatively talk when asked. John had told him to keep all transmissions as short as possible. If Officer Shepherd was true to his word, and survived the fires, they may not be welcome back in town, so John wanted to not give them a chance to locate them via transmissions.

"Hurry, come on," Linny grabbed Michael's hand and pulled him towards the section of forest where they had picked blackberries.

Checking snares, John discovered that plump rabbit had found its way into the trap. They dispatched it, and John got out his skinning knife and dressed it out right there.

"So you saw how I did that, right?" John asked Linny, who was the older of the two kids, by a little bit.

"Yes sir, you pulled his head up while holding his feet," she said, no longer grossed out by the process.

"Ok, what comes next?" John asked Bret, and the younger boy was beaming with pride over his catch.

"You cut its head off and get the guts out," Bret

replied, his expression sobering.

"Either one of you kids ready to do this?" John held up the knife. Neither kid stepped forward, so he did it himself, slow enough so they could watch.

Michael remembered the first time he'd cleaned a rabbit. John's method was similar to his own, but he'd learned to do it with the carcass flat on a cutting board. John tied the carcass upside down to a nearby branch by its hind legs, and removed the head, allowing the blood of the kill to drip. The idea there was to allow the blood to exit the carcass as quick as possible, so it didn't taint the meat.

Next, he cut off the forepaws and cut around the hind legs near the last joint. He then slit the animal from neck to groin, and made a Y-shaped incision that joined the groin to the cuts around the hind legs. John worked quickly and efficiently cutting around the tail, making sure that when he scooped the guts out he didn't nick the bladder. With that out of the way, he tested the branch and took an edge of the skin by the hind legs and peeled down. He did that to the other side until he was able to put some more weight on it where the two pieces came together below the tail.

"Ready to see how I take them off in one piece?" Bret had been asking about the process the previous day, and he smiled and nodded.

"Ok, now that the tail is down and the guts are out, you take the skin and you just pull…" John said with a grunt, and pulled the remainder of the skin off.

It came in one piece and where he'd removed the forepaws at the furthest joint, the skin slipped over and off. What he had was a skin that was complete, minus the head. One of the last things he did was untie the carcass and put it on the ground and gently cut the hind legs off. John and Michael examined the liver and kidneys for things that didn't look right, but didn't find anything more than a couple of bot fly larvae from the skin, and they could cut that out if it was still in there.

"Let's go check the hooks," Michael suggested, scooping the offal into a bucket.

They'd been using the offal and guts for fishing. Since Bret's first rabbit, the fishing had actually improved somewhat on the trotline. It was only the small variety of food that was keeping the little kids happy; their amusement at the stinky fish was quickly turning into outright loathing. Michael considered what some basics like salt and pepper would do for flavor and the kid's attitudes.

"I'll cook this guy up for breakfast. Maybe somebody on the radio knows how to tan these things?" John held up the pelt.

"Sounds good to me. I'm taking the kids out to check the lines."

"Be careful," John said, knowing Michael would be.

Michael just nodded.

CHAPTER 2

THE HOMESTEAD, KENTUCKY

Blake was playing his hundredth game of checkers for the day, using his right arm slowly. He'd gotten lucky after being shot and operated on. He kept his bedroom door open, more out of boredom and loneliness than anything else. He'd spent the quiet time since Kenny had died healing. His muscles itched as they knit themselves back together, and he had tried to stay out of everyone's way. He'd spent a good week and a half fighting off some sort of infection, but they had been able to stamp it down with the supplies that Martha had brought back from her office. The shots Martha had given him along with her constant attention to the wounds had finally won out. He felt a little out of sorts, but human for the first time in a while.

"Do you want to play another game Dad?"

BOYD CRAVEN

Chris asked Blake.

"No, I think I want to go outside for a bit," he said, and Chris's eyes got big.

Chris handed him his cane and ran for the front door yelling for Sandra and Lisa. Blake had already made it to his feet and was testing his balance with his bad leg when Sandra burst into the house, scaring Blake and David who practically lived stationed at the radio. Blake smiled at that, because it wasn't unusual for Chris to take off like the hounds of hell were on his butt, looking for a grownup to come help Blake.

"What's wrong? Do you have to go to the bathroom?" Sandra asked, walking up and wrapping her arms around his chest, mindful of his shoulder.

"No, I think I want to sit outside a bit today. I'm going crazy back there," he nodded at the bedroom.

"Well, good thing we made a bench seat out there. Come on, I'll help you," Sandra got under one of his arms, but Blake just squeezed her gently.

She looked up at him puzzled for a minute and then he leaned down, kissing her thoroughly. Her breath caught a minute and her fingers curled into the fabric of his shirt. He smiled into the kiss and broke it, watching her open her eyes and letting them come back into focus.

"Don't you start that. You're too hurt for…"

"I want to try getting around by myself. Stay close, I promise I won't try to overdo it."

"You… Ohhh you sneaky man. Ok, let's see how tough you are. Giddy up." She gave his good side a

THE WORLD BLEEDS

quick hug and then walked backwards towards the door.

With every step, Blake felt his stiff leg cry out in pain, but he felt like he needed to get out and get some fresh air. Most of his life had been spent out of doors, and he'd only come inside to sleep. The self-imposed time healing had been the hardest weeks of his life. He was ready to test things out and Martha had told him the night before that he should start to move about a bit, but slowly. Making it to the front door, Blake paused a moment, holding onto the jam. He smiled as the Kentucky sunshine washed over him and the warm fresh breeze ruffled his hair. The bench he found on the front was one of Bobby's designs and Sandra took the cane and helped him sit so he wouldn't have to bend his stiff leg too much. It was his shoulder that hurt the most though, when he rotated his arm. The pain went away slowly and he sat back and smiled.

Blake knew about the changes to the homestead, but what he wasn't prepared for was the number of people he could see. The grass was still tall around the homestead, but it had paths worn through it to and from the barn, and children played in the designated safe zone between them, staying away from the toe poppers. It had been a concern, but when the kids understood the gravity of the situation they agreed.

It felt good to Blake, to see kids laughing, and Chris and one of the kids they had rescued from the slavers were throwing a red kickball around.

Sandra sat beside him and wrapped an arm around his good side, curled into her husband.

"You know, if the world hadn't decided to tear itself apart, I'd almost think I was in heaven."

Sandra smiled at him. "I know. Sgt. Smith says we have a pretty clear area around here for now. My squad has been cross training with his men and…"

"It's going to be hard to have the guys called back to base, huh?" Blake smiled.

"Well, most of the ladies are single, except for Melissa. I think Bobby still has to watch out for Curt, but other than that…"

"What's the story on their base or central command or whatever?"

"You don't remember me telling you?" she asked, puzzled.

"No, I remember endless board games with Chris and lying awake at night because my sleep is so screwy. I remember we talked about it, but the details are fuzzy."

"Painkillers?" Sandra asked him.

"Only the first week or so," he told her.

"Makes sense. Well, they got no response. None, until a week ago. When they called into their regular frequency to check in, somebody else answered. Smith says they had a foreign sounding accent."

"Wow, so the invasion thing Patty was talking about…?"

"I don't know for sure," Sandra admitted.

They both looked up as the door opened and

THE WORLD BLEEDS

Patty stepped out and sat on the floor of the porch, leaning into a support pole.

"I heard my name," Patty said, meeting Sandra's eyes.

"I was just telling Blake about the boys, and the voices on the radio."

Patty was silent and then she looked at Blake and gave him a small smile. "You know, when I first met you I thought you were mostly dead. You don't look too bad, all things considered."

"I'm glad you and Neal were able to…" Blake paused, realizing that he'd said the dead man's name aloud. He knew that Neal was someone special to her, and he hadn't meant to poke a sore spot, but she just continued to smile. "What I'm saying is, I'm grateful that you two saved me. I'm truly sorry for your loss," Blake finished.

"Thank you for taking me in. I know I haven't been pulling my weight around here. I just don't know what to do." Patty said, starting to pick at her fingernails.

"Did somebody tell you that?" Blake asked a little pointedly and Patty jerked her gaze up to meet his eyes again.

"No, it's just that everybody has a job around here and now with the soldiers here, more and more people are coming in. All I've been doing is moping around in the basement."

"Patty, you know you're welcome to work with me and the ladies in the squad," Sandra told her.

"Before losing Neal, I might have taken you up

on that. The day he died I think part of me did too. I don't think I'm cut out for fighting and danger the way you folks are. I don't think I can survive out here without someone like you to…"

The tears came hard and fast and Sandra untangled herself from Blake's side and sat on the edge of the porch next to Patty. She put her arm around the young lady's shoulders and hugged her. Sandra smoothed down her hair as Patty buried her head on her shoulder.

"You know, not everyone is cut out for fighting. There's nothing wrong with that, and look at my mother in law. She isn't a fighter either. What I don't want you to do though is think that you have to pay your way into staying here," Sandra looked to Blake for confirmation, but he was already nodding to her.

"If you are looking for something to do, or to feel like you can contribute more, maybe you can help learn the radio setups from David. Right now only Sgt. Smith, David and I use them more than the hand held units."

"What'd David do, you know, before?" Patty asked, perhaps trying to change the subject.

"He got caught up with some bad dudes," Blake told her, "but you know that story."

"No, I mean, before that? If I'm going to work with him…" Patty's voice trailed off.

"I don't know, how about you go find out?" Sandra said, squeezing her shoulder one more time before standing and stepping off the porch.

THE WORLD BLEEDS

"You know, I probably will. Thank you, both of you." Patty stood and headed back into the house.

"You going to stay right there Mr. Jackson?" Sandra asked, giving Blake 'The Look'.

"Yes ma'am. If I need anything, I'll have Chris let you know. You heading off?"

"Yeah, the squad and Sgt. Smith's guys are going to go through town again and search for survivors. We've also found two more food trucks to empty."

"You stay safe." Blake said, feeling a stab of anxiety.

"You bet." She smiled before heading off.

§ § §

Blake sat there for a long while and, once the day started to get warm, David came out with a glass of iced tea for him. Lisa wandered in with Duncan to check in on him, and Duncan helped Blake make sure he didn't fall going to the bathroom before helping him back outside. They both commented that his color looked better. After eating a quick bite, Chris introduced him to the new folks from the homestead who had been keeping their distance, but one by one they started to approach him as he sat outside.

Their stories both amazed him and saddened him. It was stories of loss and love, blood pain and pure joy. He had just about every faction of America right on the ten acres he owned. He found out that his garden hadn't been neglected, but had been enlarged and taken over by several of the men and women. With foraging parties coming and going, more folks had been brought back to the homestead and they were introduced to Blake by Duncan. The entire afternoon went on like that, until the radio on Duncan's waist squawked. He put the ear bud in and listened, replied and told the folks within earshot to follow him.

"Squad's back, they have a load of food or two."

"Or two?" Blake asked, surprised.

"Well, there were two food trucks. We found an old diesel tractor trailer at Prichard's farm. Old beast fired right up after we got the water out of the lines. We've had it stashed for a few days now. The plan was to drag the trailers close to the homestead, then ferry them up with the small trucks. We'll dump the trailers afterwards, but that was your wife, calling to tell me the first one was parked outside Holloway Lane."

"Isn't that like ringing the dinner bell to every raider, bandit or creep in the area?"

"There really aren't any left." Duncan said.

Blake was shocked. "What? How is that?"

"We've been keeping an eye on things. People around here keep their heads down when we come through and our group is big enough now that it isn't really a worry... but... That's why we're moving the trailers as soon as they are unloaded. Don't worry. I've got about three or four soldiers that stayed back watching over the perimeter."

"Okay. That sounds good then." Blake told his

THE WORLD BLEEDS

father in law.

It was ok, but the mess of pain meds and healing had left Blake feeling out of touch with everything that had been going on. Things had changed and, although it was all things he'd agree with anyways, he felt a little left out. Part of that was the loneliness talking and part of it was the pain, but he vowed to keep his wits and got his cane. He headed inside slowly. He smiled when he saw Patty with the headset on, one ear free while David explained the basics of the radio systems they used.

"Hi Blake, need a chair?" David scrambled to his feet.

"That'd be great," He told David, who pulled one out from under the kitchen table and brought it to him, setting it down by the radio.

Blake sat a little less gracefully than he'd have liked, but the chair held up to him plopping down. It hurt a bit, but slowly the muscles were loosening up.

"What's on the radio?" Blake asked.

"We're listening in on a group that's organizing an attack to free folks from a FEMA camp. The camp knows it's coming but they can't get anybody to come help." Patty said, and something about her voice made Blake look at her.

It was confidence. Anybody could tell she was nervous but maybe all she needed was purpose to go on, to heal her broken soul. Blake knew it couldn't happen overnight, but it looked like she had taken a step in the right direction.

"FEMA Camp? Why are folks attacking it? If the folks want out, can't they just leave?" Blake asked.

"Blake, there's been a lot going on," David began, and Blake sat there and soaked all the new information in until his wife returned, an armload of supplies in her hands.

"No food?" Blake asked her, puzzled.

"No, we're storing that in the cellar, this is body wash, shampoo, razors... Oh and here's some scissors." Sandra told him, running her hands through his hair.

"You going to give me a haircut or something?" he asked her, smiling.

"Haircut, shave, sponge bath," she waggled her eyebrows and Blake almost tipped his chair over trying to stand.

David laughed and steadied the chair as Blake stood.

"Easy killer, I said bath, not shenanigans," Sandra said with a sly smile.

Patty turned slightly pink but smiled and dropped a wink to Sandra, who returned the look with a smirk.

CHAPTER 3

PINHOTI TRAIL, ALABAMA

S o, what do you think? Is it worth it?" Michael
asked John.

"Yeah… I mean, the kids' clothing is
wearing out. Their shoes are shot."

"I know I keep pushing for this John, but…"
Michael stammered, but his words cut off with
John's laughter.

"There's no way to know what's out there, but
I am ready to go too. Even though we lived in the
sticks, we didn't live like this," John motioned to the
campsite.

"So we pack it up?"

"Yeah, let's give it a day to pack up and we'll
head out tomorrow morning."

§ § §

It didn't take the four of them long to pack up the campsite. Linny was the one who did most of the work, pulling in the trotline, and they only kept one large fish from the day so they could have a light meal before heading out in the morning. What to take and what to leave took more thinking out loud between Michael and John than they expected. They also considered one of them going and the other watching the kids but, in the end, they decided to stick together.

The kids were excited at first, but as they hiked, they became quiet and somber. John had told them what they could expect, as much as possible. They stopped to use the bathrooms, which hadn't been touched surprisingly, but none of the water worked.

"I miss my Dad," Linny said quietly as she looked at their car which now sat on a flat tire, giving it an off balance look.

"Me too," Bret said.

Michael didn't say anything, but decided to walk ahead a little bit, to avoid the chatter. He still felt guilty, and hadn't been able to tell the kids that he was the one who killed their father. The guilt gnawed away at him at odd moments. He tried to comfort himself by saying it was in self-defense, and it was, but the guilt remained.

"You go on ahead and check out the car," John said before Michael was out of earshot.

"Yeah, I won't be long."

"You have a round in the chamber?" John asked.

Michael turned and walked backwards a

moment. He pulled the slide on the .45 back a little bit then nodded. He holstered his father's pistol again, and patted his back pocket, checking for the two spare magazines. In the end, Michael had elected to keep most of his supplies at the camp, bringing only his daypack, some water bottles, his grandpa's old grease gun with a ton of extra ammo, and all the spare magazines.

"You know what, take this. I'm not sure if I can use it," Michael said, stripping off the M2 and handing it to John.

John nodded, and understood the pain the young man was still struggling with. It turned out that Michael had been a natural with the .45, but if he'd at least shot the M2 before John would have argued for the young man to keep it. As it was, he knew Michael would wear out faster carrying the carbine than John would.

"Okay. You going to be all right?"

"Yeah, it's just—" Michael looked at the kids and turned and walked again until he was almost out of sight.

"Is Michael sad about our dad too?" Linny asked.

"I think so. Come on, let's stick together."

§ § §

Michael reached the Impala long before they did, and pulled the brush off the green tarp they'd used to cover it. Once he had that clear, he folded the tarp, fished the keys out of his pocket, and put the tarp and his pack in the trunk. The explosive heat almost made him wince. He knew the interior would be almost as bad, so he opened the doors and rolled down the windows. He didn't want to start it right away, knowing that everybody for miles would hear the throaty grumble of his motor. He just never got around to fixing that exhaust leak, making it sound like a like a hotrod to the kids in his class.

Now, the thought of making that much noise made him nervous. The car was a magical instrument of travel; one more thing they'd taken for granted, until either nothing worked, or it made you a target like it had with the late Chief. The conversation about his old girlfriend's father was another he was dreading if it ever came up. Almost against his will, he started to hum '*I shot the sheriff*', knowing he'd had no other choice there, either. Suddenly 17 felt a lot younger than he'd felt before and, not for the first time, he wished his parents were there somewhere. He'd love to talk to his Dad.

"Did the lights turn on when you opened the doors?" John asked, emerging from the roadside.

"Yeah, I think we should be fine. Want to store your stuff in the trunk?" Michael asked John.

"No, I'll keep it with me. Do you uh… Think we should go back for a booster or something?" John asked looking at Bret's smiling face when he saw the car.

"If we're pulled over, I expect we'll have bigger problems than the booster seat," Michael said soberly, then realized the question was something of a joke.

John smiled and held up his hand for the keys.

"But…"

"If things get hairy, I'm trained to drive like the devil. It's safer."

Michael grinned and tossed him the keys before opening his door and let the kids into the backseat.

"If he's driving like the devil, you both better put on your seatbelts," Michael said.

"I said if things get hairy—" John started to say.

"But you are hairy," Linny spoke up.

"I'm putting my belt on," Bret said, making them all laugh.

John threw his hands up in mock surrender and fired up the car when everyone was buckled in. The throaty V8 made itself heard, and John goosed the gas pedal until the motor ran smoothly. They put the car in gear and started their way slowly towards Choccolocco. The closer they got to the town, the quieter they all got. John pointed out the window and tendrils of smoke rising from the distance.

"What's that smell?" Linny asked, her voice tiny in the backseat, almost too quiet to hear over the Impala's open exhaust.

"I don't know kiddo," John lied.

They could all smell it, and John shared a look with Michael. The smell was of decay, like the time they had left a pile of fish guts out in the sun and forgot to throw the rest into the lake to chum. Within a couple days they found the pile again by smell, and it was horrid in the Alabama heat. They had scraped it into a hastily dug hole and covered it. This smell was like that.

"Where are we headed first?" Michael asked John, as they rolled into town.

"Let's go check out our houses. See if—"

"Yeah." Michael replied.

"Do you guys have more games for my DS?" Brett asked.

"I do, but it isn't going to work," Michael said, leaning back to look over the front seats.

"I know," Bret said in a huff, "Just checking."

"Hey, somebody broke those houses," Linny said pointing out a sight that had both men wincing already.

The houses in their neighborhood were shells of what they once were. It wasn't the big fires that had ruined them, but people by the looks of things. Michael's front door was busted off its hinges and the garage door was up. They pulled into the driveway.

"Oh man." John said as he turned off the motor and got the M2 out with him. "You stay with the kids for a sec, would ya?"

"It's my house," Michael protested, stepping out of the car and pulling his .45.

"Just stick by the car, ok?"

"All right," Michael said and John entered through the broken front door.

"Is Uncle John going to be right back?" Linny asked through an open side window.

THE WORLD BLEEDS

"Yeah, he's a pretty tough dude." Michael told her and reached in to muss her hair.

"Your garage is all messy. My Dad doesn't have a messy garage like that," Bret said.

Michael had realized that already. Somebody or somebodies had torn through there. His rolling tool chest was still there, but every drawer was open and all the tools were missing. Boxes that had been stacked on wire shelving were open and clothes he'd outgrown were strewn around. The door that connected to the house was open and, without moving from beside the car, he could see large holes punched through the sheetrock.

"Your house didn't look like this when you left, did it?" Linny asked.

Michael was choked up. He could only imagine what the rest of the house looked like, and all he kept thinking about was what would his parents think.

"*Did they make it back here to find this? I should have left them a note. I wish I'd said more than a quick goodbye.*" The thoughts kept playing over and over in Michael's head, and the kids' questions fell silent as they realized he wasn't listening anymore. John appeared in the connecting doorway, and he was looking at Michael with apologetic eyes.

"It's pretty trashed in there. Somebody was looking for food and..." John broke off as they heard motors heading their way.

"Oh shit," John muttered running for the car.

Instead of jumping in, he turned the key and put

the car in neutral. Michael immediately understood the play and opened the passenger door and pushed. Bret and Linny slid out and Bret went to the back of the car and pushed. Linny stood there puzzled for a second, until finally the big Impala moved with the combined weight of the three of them. As soon as the rear bumper passed the garage door tracks, John gave a hoarse yell to Linny to pull the cord down.

She snapped out of her confusion and was able to get the door in place. The rumble of the steel door coming down wouldn't have normally been alarming, but suddenly it was the loudest noise besides whatever was coming their way.

"Do you think they saw us?" Michael whispered.

"I don't know. Did you see what it was?" John asked him, going to a small window in the garage door and looking out to either side."

"No, I didn't see anything. It happened so fast." Michael replied.

They stood there in the dark and Bret worked his way next to Michael, fitting his small hand into the older boy's. Michael gave the hand a squeeze and pulled Linny close in a one-armed hug. The sound grew closer and everyone fell silent, hoping they hadn't been noticed.

CHAPTER 4

HOMESTEAD, KENTUCKY

It had been close to two weeks and Blake slowly regained his strength. His shoulder and arm weren't worth much, but he was finally able to leave the porch and travel around the homestead on his bum leg. Chris suggested they keep one of the quads nearby for him, so the Four-Trax was set aside for him. Everybody at the homestead was busy. There were more people on the property than he even knew what to do with. Duncan and Sandra had been working on scheduling things; everyone knew that winter was on its way, and the two squads of soldiers were proving invaluable for their manpower and firepower.

Firewood was cut, some by chainsaw, some with hand tools and the one hundred years' worth of tools and junk in the barn. Blake's kitchen was always full, with somebody running the canner. Outside the house in the shade, an area had been shoveled flat by the French drains, and many propane burners were set up. The same portable kind that folks used as turkey fryers. Supplies could be found in town and they started a seven man party to scavenge, scout and look for survivors. Several of the local pharmacies were emptied, although the pain killers and psych medications had already been looted. Stockpiles of supplies were collected.

If survivors were found, they were checked over by one of soldiers who'd been an EMT in a former life. If anything serious came up, Martha was called, or the survivor was brought closer to the homestead and Martha came out to meet with them. More than that though, they all kept an ear out. Chatter started to fill the military channels and none of the men recognized the call signs of the foreign sounding voices. Whenever they tried to contact their commanding officers, they were ordered to return to their guard unit's armory for re-assignment. The problem was, none of them believed what they were hearing.

All the hustle and bustle had Blake itching to jump in, but he still couldn't. Some days he ended up sitting on his porch with Chris, playing a board game until one of the other kids came up to have him come play. When that happened, Blake would head inside and sit with David and Patty. They usually unplugged their headphones so he could listen in on what was going on. It was on a day like this that he found a new outlet for his creativity that had been sitting dormant, awaiting his help.

"Hello?" A young woman's voice came out of the radio, clear and without distortion, "Can anybody hear me?"

Patty grabbed the transmitter and spoke, "I can hear you, are you ok?"

"Yeah, I just found this radio and decided to try it out. Dumb luck, huh?"

"Yeah, I guess it is. Is it a big radio?"

"Oh no, it's a hand held radio. I found it under a dead soldier. I thought it was a weird thing to hold on to since all the electronics died..."

"From what we can tell, most military radio pieces work fine, but tell me," Patty paused and looked at the men, "why was the soldier dead?"

"It was from the group that got into a gunfight with the bikers out here."

"Where's here?"

"Charlotte. Listen, I have to go find some water somewhere. I'll be back later on. It's nice talking to people who aren't out to hurt me."

"Thanks. I'm Patty. I'll be right here."

"Thanks Patty, call me Z."

"Z?"

"I have a weird name." Z said.

"Ask her if she knows about the water heaters?" Blake said, becoming interested.

"Hey Z, real quick, do you know about water heaters?" Patty asked, her expression puzzled as she looked at Blake.

"No, what about them? They quit working when the gas quit."

Blake grabbed the microphone and pressed the transmit button.

"This is Blake, the water heater is still a holding tank. There's a valve at the bottom for maintenance. I'm willing to bet if you're around a ton of empty houses you can find one or two that are full. That's probably more water than you'd need…"

"I have to go," Z said and the radio went silent except for a little feedback.

"Wow, I never would have thought of that, Blake," David said standing up and stretching. "You want my seat for a bit? I'm going to head to the barracks and see if Ms. Corinne's sourdough starter worked."

"Sure," Blake said, scooting closer to the radio.

"But what about me? I don't—" Patty started to say in a panicked voice.

"You'll do fine, besides, the squad and guard units have their own communications gear now. We've just got a bigger reach with this base unit and antenna system they rigged up."

Patty took a deep breath and nodded, and David headed out.

"You know how to run this?" Patty asked Blake.

"Somewhat. I haven't done much with it though."

"Hey, uh… Blake, this is Z." The voice came out of the radio, but you could tell she was whispering.

"Go ahead, I'm still here."

THE WORLD BLEEDS

"I think you saved me. I haven't had water for a day and a half now. I'm in somebody's basement and found it just like you said. Thank you."

"No problem. Just call back on this channel if you need to brainstorm or talk or—"

"Blake," a new voice came out of the radio, cutting him off, "Thanks for the tip also, it's something… Oops, my lady says I just walked all over your transmission. Thanks!"

Three other voices spoke up, calling in from across the country, one by one thanking him. Blake was shocked and surprised.

"Maybe you should do this more often?" Patty said, a rare smile tugging at the corners of her mouth.

"Yeah, I agree," Lisa said, and they turned to see her coming out of the kitchen, mitts on her hands from handling the canners.

"We need a name for it, something cool," Patty was all out smiling now.

"Guerilla Radio?" Lisa suggested, pulling the mitts off and walking over to Blake.

"Why Guerilla Radio?" Blake asked his mother in law.

"I don't know. Rage Against the Machine had this song and it reminded me of it." Lisa said.

Patty cracked up as she looked up at Lisa. "Rage Against the Machine? You?"

"Yeah, me. What?"

Blake chuckled, "I'm not sure it needs a name."

"Hey, world, what do you think of the name,

Guerilla Radio for a regularly scheduled broadcast on tips and help? An old school radio version of the internet or Wikipedia?" Patty said into the mic.

"Rebel Radio!" Z's voice came through loud and clear.

Her sentiments were echoed by more voices than had called in earlier and, when a familiar voice got on, Blake sat up, his smile even bigger.

"Blake, hon, I think it's a great idea. Let's find an unused frequency and we'll start sharing it with the world," Sandra urged.

"Rebel Radio?" Blake asked.

"Sounds like a plan," Patty said, looking to Lisa.

"Rebel Radio." Lisa agreed.

CHAPTER 5

CHOCCOLOCCO, ALABAMA

D o you think they saw us?" Michael whispered.

"I don't think so... Bret and Linny, if you see or hear someone you don't know, stick close to one of us got it?"

"Got it," they chorused nervously.

Michael peeped outside. "Those don't look like the normal APCs the cops in the big cities have been getting."

"That's because they aren't. Those were Russian built BTR-80s." John said, his voice strained.

"The Russians are invading us? Is this like *Red Dawn*?" Michael asked.

"No, they quit making those a long time back. They're like the cockroaches of the APC world. Everybody has a few and they just don't die. Black

31

market sales when their economy tanked—"

They fell silent as the sounds of motors could be heard again and Michael felt a tug on his hand. Bret was holding himself and stepping from one foot to another silently.

"I really have to go," Bret almost pleaded.

"Ok. John, can you keep an eye out?"

John nodded and Michael led Bret into the house. He turned when he heard a crunch behind him and saw that Linny was following them.

"I have to go too," she said.

Michael led them to the main bathroom. It had been trashed, the medicine cabinet torn out of the wall, its contents spilled all over. He pointed to the toilet and then to Bret, and led Linny to his parents' bedroom where there was a master bath.

"When you're done, meet me in the hallway," he whispered, and she nodded before shutting the door.

Michael had to go himself, and he wasn't sure if it was from hearing the sound of those motors or the fact he really had to go. He waited in the hallway and Bret opened the door to the guest bath.

"Toilet doesn't flush," he whispered.

"That's ok, wait here for me and your sister."

Michael closed the door and held his breath while he went. He slowly counted to ten until sweet relief. He was almost done when a firm knock on the door startled him.

"I'll be right out," he said, not quite whispering.

"You have to hurry, they're coming." John's

THE WORLD BLEEDS

voice was frantic.

Michael opened the door and looked out. John had always been calm and laid back. When the standoff with the police happened, he'd never lost his cool.

"There's two of them out front, the APCs are a little further down the street. I want you to take the kids and head out back, go to my place. I'm going to distract them."

"How?"

"I need your car," John said and Michael nodded.

They both knew the car couldn't stand up to the rolling war machines they'd seen, but with any luck, whoever was out there had no idea how many people were inside. Those machine guns could cut the car in half... Despite that, it wasn't a bad plan. And it was the only plan.

"If I can't find you by my house, make your way back to the cave when this is all done."

"John, I... Thanks." Michael said and hugged his friend's father, a man he'd now come to associate as more than that, much more.

"Go! Hurry," John motioned to the back door.

Michael and the kids darted out, using the privacy fence for cover until they reached the back. Michael stood on his tip toes and looked into the neighbors' yard, not seeing anything. He boosted the kids over, letting them fall softly. Suddenly, the roar of Michael's Impala shook the house. A screeching of metal made Michael wince and then tires squealed as it took off. Immediately, the revving of the APCs could be heard, followed by a long string of automatic gunfire. Michael scampered up and over the fence as quick as he could, grabbing the kids' hands and heading for the next yard, trying to put distance between them.

"In here, quick," Michael pointed to the corner of the shrubbery.

The neighbor had taken meticulous care of his lawn and shrubs, working the back of them into a hedge of sorts. Michael had been hired off and on to take care of this lawn and do the gardening when the old man wasn't around and knew that in the corner there was a hollow spot where shrubs met up. It was there he hid the kids and he wedged himself in beside them.

"What do we do now?" Linny asked.

"I don't know. Shhhh, let's listen."

Michael could still hear his car's distinctive rumble, but it was moving away and getting quieter.

"Maybe John'll be ok," Bret said, a quiver in his voice.

§ § §

John's hasty exit tore the garage door free as the Detroit muscle pushed its way past. He braked hard, the remains of the door slid off, and he shifted into drive, peeling rubber. A quick glance in the side mirror showed the coaxial machine gun turning in his direction. John pushed the pedal down harder

THE WORLD BLEEDS

and tore out of the immediate area as the APCs started to move. He winced when he heard the chatter of automatic weapons and watched sparks erupt from the road beside him.

"*They aren't shooting at me, they're trying to get me to stop*," John thought and made a hard turn down the road that led to the interstate. He started to weave the car from side to side as the machine gun hosed rounds at the car. He knew the APC had a top speed of close to 50mph, so he did his best to push Michael's car up to speeds far above that, until the men in the APC decided he wasn't getting the picture.

The lead APC opened up with its bigger gun, punching holes through the passenger side, and smoke erupted from under the engine compartment. John could see a sharp turn coming up and didn't want to slow much, so as he got close, he pulled the parking brake and floored it while turning the wheel. It had been many years since John had had to use the defensive driving skills that he'd learned in the teams, but they hadn't grown too rusty, and he got the car pointed down the center of the road again. John took half a second to check the gauges because the smoke or steam was increasing - and he never saw the truck that rammed the driver's side.

The truck had been a deuce and a half, or one of its variants. The heavy metal bumper crumpled the side door and John's vehicle rolled as the passenger side tire crumpled. It tumbled and he was thrown around the inside of the car. His vision dimmed as he hit his head several times.

The door being wrenched open was what made him come to. A fresh-faced young man, no older than his early twenties, was speaking to him. John couldn't hear what he was saying and his head was spinning. The man pulled John out and dragged him by his arms into the underbrush.

"Don't talk," the stranger said, pulling branches over John.

John couldn't if he wanted to, but the voice of the stranger was funny. It had a foreign accent somehow, but his English was clear.

They sat like that for a minute, and eventually the driver of the deuce and a half got out with a crimson smear from his nose to neck. He was pinching the bridge of his nose and screaming orders into a hand held radio in a foreign language. Seconds passed and the APCs caught up with the tangled mess of car and truck. Six troops got out of the two APCs and met up with the bloody man.

"I do not know… I hit my face on the wheel…"

"I did not want him dead! You were to block…"

"Dirty Americans, they did this to themselves…"

"…want to clean up their mess. Yosef, you and your team fan out. He may be armed."

"Come, they will find us if we stay here," the stranger said, pulling on John's arm.

"Who are you?" John asked, trying to fight down the nausea and blinding pain in his forehead.

"Henrikas, formerly of Lithuania's armed forces. Hurry, they will kill me if they find me, you they

THE WORLD BLEEDS

will just interrogate. Then kill you," he said with a smile.

"Henrikas?"

"Yes, please, we must hurry."

"Lead the way, Henry," John said getting to his feet with less grace than he would have liked.

§ § §

Michael could kick himself. They had been safe in the hedgerow until they moved into John's yard to see if he'd returned. His house had been trashed just like Michael's parents' house had and the rear door was off its hinges. Michael and the kids crept inside and peered around.

"John?" Michael asked softly, Bret holding his hand and Linny holding onto his shirt tail.

"Please, step in," he heard, but it wasn't John's voice. He turned to run, but three men with carbines had them covered. Michael looked back towards the direction of the voice when another soldier stepped forward, his carbine at the ready, but not aimed at them.

"Please, we aren't going to hurt these children. Lower your weapons," he had a smooth cultured voice.

The soldiers complied and Michael's eyebrows rose when he noticed the NATO armband. Things clicked into place and he relaxed slightly, but he worried about John.

"Thank you, we were stopping at my house to

look for things. I didn't know that…"

"Your country has had martial law enacted. Did you not know this?"

"Just what we heard on the old radio," Michael said as both kids got on either side of him and held onto him tightly.

"I am sorry for earlier, we heard a motor that we suspected belonged to a criminal faction operating around here. The motor sounded as loud as our personnel carriers so we thought—"

"I heard guns," Linny said in a small voice.

"Yes, your friend, he surprised my men. We were trying to get him to stop."

"Is he ok?"

The man hesitated for a second too long and Michael pulled the kids tight and tried to take a step backwards, right into the men standing behind him. He moved forward again, feeling Bret crushing his hand in a tight grip.

"He hit one of our trucks trying to run. He was, how do you say it… getting the lead out, when the car crashed."

"Is he—"

"We did not find him. There is no blood inside of the car but the windshield was gone. We spent an hour looking to see if he was thrown clear."

"He's gone?" Bret asked, his voice hitching.

Michael looked down and saw fat tears pooling up in the boys eyes. He knelt and picked up Bret who put his arms around his neck and buried his face into his shoulder.

THE WORLD BLEEDS

"We did not find a body. We will, of course, keep searching. I am Commander Lukashenko, and I insist you three come with me."

"Where are we going?" Michael asked, feeling like something dropped into the pit of his stomach making him both nauseous and stone cold afraid of the answer.

"We have a camp for survivors, you will be safer there until your military can return home and some semblance of order restored," the Commander said.

"Do we have to go far, sir?" Linny asked, and the Commander gave her a big smile.

"No dear, it's been set up about thirty miles away. We can transport you there easily. Is there anything you'd like to take from your house here before we leave?"

"*Maybe this won't be so bad after all,*" Michael thought to himself, "*This is our friend John's house. The one who was driving...*"

"Ah yes, so the house where you first parked is yours, yes?" Lukashenko asked, his voice smooth.

"Yes," Michael replied.

"Good, my men will take you there, then we shall leave. Is there anyone else in the area that could benefit from our help?"

Michael was ready to say no but the way Commander Lukashenko paused and said help with a sarcastic smile made him cold. "No sir."

"Good, good. We will, of course, need to confiscate your guns."

CHAPTER 6

Choccolocco, Alabama

John woke for the second day in a row with what felt like the world's worst hangover. He rolled over before he could puke on himself and dry heaved on the floor of the barn they had been hiding in. Henrikas had immediately recognized the severity of the concussion and had led John out of the area before they had been found. He'd helped him into the barn before collapsing with exhaustion from dragging John several miles as he drifted in and out of consciousness.

"Good, you are awake again," he said, handing a steaming mug to John.

"Barely," John said, taking the mug, "How long?" They both knew what he was asking.

"Two days, you are still in rough shape."

"Why?"

THE WORLD BLEEDS

"Why?" Henrikas asked.

"Why did you help me?"

"Because like you, I am a fugitive – but for other reasons."

John pondered that for a moment, "Why am I a fugitive? We did nothing wrong."

"You are… were… Let me find the words… You should have already been in the camps. All people that the troops can find are in the camps." Henrikas grabbed a steaming mug from his feet and motioned for John to drink.

The broth was salty and for a moment his stomach almost rebelled but he knew he needed to hold it down. Two days was a long time to be in and out of things. John almost scalded himself when his stomach accepted the broth, and it begged for more. It was all he could do not to drink the whole mug in one shot.

"So, you and the troops. You're with the UN?"

"Some of us. I was conscripted many years ago and, when we heard that our unit was coming to America to help rebuild, I was happy. But things were not as they seemed."

"How so?" John asked him, finishing the mug and sitting it down.

"The Navy, your boats and submarines, ya?" Henrikas asked and John nodded, "They have been fighting almost nonstop. Boats, airplanes and all sorts of peoples were trying to come here. Many made it, your Navy sank many more or shot down the airplanes. They have been too busy trying to keep ISIS away. Much of the world is now at war as your cruise missiles have turned entire countries into smoking piles of glass. Your president and vice president came out of hiding to speak with... ambassadors? Heads of state? The area was hit by a small yield nuclear bomb. We do not know who set it off."

John let those words digest before asking, "So where do you and the UN fit in with this?"

Henrikas shrugged. "I do not know much more than that, except that the peacekeeping we were supposed to be helping and supporting is basically to throw Americans into camps. I had always planned on defecting if possible, but what I saw in those camps and what the world is allowing to happen to America, it only pushed my agenda to happen faster. I left my post three weeks ago."

The two of them talked off and on that day as Henrikas kept making broth, and then a thin stew when it became apparent that John was past the worst of the nausea. The constant worry for Michael and the kids kept gnawing at him. Neither of them knew what had happened to them.

"I have to go back to the house and see if they're there," John told Henrikas, or Henry as he'd started to call him. "If not there, maybe they are back at the camp we stayed in," he had been careful to not disclose how they'd survived the past month or where.

"It is possible the Commander has moved onto the Anniston area, but he still has patrols that sweep through the countryside. If we are careful… My friend, I do not want to get caught, but my conscience won't allow me to sit idle anymore. I pray they are there and not in the camps."

John silently agreed, but just nodded and took a short walk to relieve himself, noting that he was still dizzy. Henrikas stood to join him but sat back down. John smiled to himself when he wasn't followed. He mostly believed his new friend, but belief wasn't blind trust. Allowing John to walk out of his sight meant at least there was some there.

"Maybe he really does have a guilty conscience, why else would he be so helpful? God, that's paranoid." John thought to himself.

He made his way back to the spot where they had camped out inside the barn only to find it empty. He found a note by where they were sitting, "Will return shortly, getting some items for tomorrow."

§ § §

TALLADEGA FEDERAL PENITENTIARY & TEMPORARY FEMA CAMP, ALABAMA

The camp was nothing like Michael thought it was going to be like; it was worse. His eye was still almost swollen closed. As soon as he was off the transport, they separated the kids from him. He'd tried to make the guards understand that they wanted to stay together, and he'd caught a rifle butt and was dragged to the men's barracks. The blow hurt more than he'd like to admit, but it really didn't scramble him the way he'd pretended. He'd been in fistfights that hurt more, but the swelling was worse for a lack of ice.

They took him into a brick building with jail style rooms on either side. A large area that looked like it used to be a cafeteria had been converted into a bunkhouse of sorts with bunk beds set up in orderly rows. Men milled about and the noise of the chatter was loud but constant, like being at a baseball game or the races before the engines fired up.

Right away, he'd noticed the condition of the men there and the stink of unwashed bodies. They were pale and thin, and many of them had a gleam in their eyes that made him feel uncomfortable. Michael wondered if his swollen eye made him look vulnerable, weak. His question was immediately answered.

"Hey kid. Your shoes, I don't have shoes that nice," a man with a rough northern accent surprised him, coming towards him from his left side.

"Yeah, they're nice." Michael said, turning slightly.

The man's skin was slightly sagging around his neck and he shuffled forward on bare feet that had rags tied around the arches. He had something shiny in his hand that he kept low to his side.

"I said, I don't have shoes that nice," The man brought the shiny object out in front of him and switched hands with it.

It looked like the handle to a fork or spoon that had been sharpened crudely to a point.

"You like my shoes?" Michael asked, in disbelief.

Things went from bad to worse in moments for Michael, and he was having a hard time processing what was going on. His entire focus went to the shank and the man's movements, but his mind was reliving the encounter in the woods, hearing that sickening crunch as he caved in a man's skull… The cries he listened to at night as the kids worried about their father. The fact the guy was trying to rob him flew right over his already sore head as he focused on the weapon.

"Kid, I'd give him your shoes if you don't want any trouble," a stranger said, coming up slightly behind the would be robber, "otherwise I think this rat fink is going to try something. We can always get them back for you later," he said with a hint of a smile.

"Shut up," the man with the shank snarled, "I don't have any shoes, the kid looks like a good match for me."

"You aren't taking my shoes," Michael said, his brain locking back into the present.

He rubbed the side of his head and moved his feet from side to side as the man with the shank moved his hand that held it in a circular fashion. He took a step closer to Michael, and when Michael was almost ready to dart to one side a dark blur made both of them flinch.

BOYD CRAVEN

The black man must have been close to three hundred pounds and a good six feet tall. He was built like a professional football player, but moved as quick and agile as a fencer. He wasn't starved or malnourished like many of the men in this room, and his raw power was enough that when his shoulder rammed the man with the shank, he flew off his feet, hitting a bunk with his upper back. The man's hands went limp and the shank fell. He was grabbed by the belt and the scruff of his shirt and slammed into the wall next to the bed and allowed to fall down in a heap. The black man smiled at Michael and knelt down to get the shank, which he promptly put in his sock.

"Thanks for the shank kid," he said and walked out of the main room into an individual cell.

Michael struggled to get his heart rate to come down from the ceiling and took a large gasping breath. The small semi-circle of men started to break up when the man who had called the other a rat fink came forward.

"I'm Les. I don't want you to think this kind of thing is normal here. I usually keep things quiet, but Jeff over there already had the shank out and none of us wanted to get poked."

"Les, hi. I'm uh… Michael. Thanks for uh… distracting him. Is he dead?" Michael asked, his attention divided between the two men, one standing and one not moving.

"He might be. I'm glad the kids aren't in this area, that would have been bad for them to see."

46

THE WORLD BLEEDS

"Kids? I've got some kids that came in with me. Where are they kept?" Michael asked.

"You're too young to have your own kids."

"I uh… They sort of grew on me. I've been taking care of them after their father died."

"Ahhh, gotcha," Les smiled and tapped Michael on the shoulder. Michael struggled not to flinch, but it was difficult.

"They're keeping the kids in the old main office building. They have it much nicer than we do. You'll see them outside sometimes. Hell, sometimes the guys and the kids all get to go out together. I think it depends on how many guards they have on duty and how bad the families are complaining." Les told him.

"What's the story on the big guy?" Michael asked, knowing that all this information would be crucial somehow.

"That's King, he was in here before."

"Before?" Michael asked, confused.

"This was a federal prison. He was in here before the balloon went up. He's one bad dude. They say he's in here for murder and he killed more while he was locked up here. If you want to survive, I'd stay away from his bad side."

The moaning on the floor distracted them both and the man got to his feet shakily, his eyes not even opening as he felt his body for injuries.

"Jeff, you stupid son of a… You know what? Michael, meet Jeff, Jeff meet—" Les started to say, but he stopped when Michael sucker punched the man in the kidney.

Jeff fell making a gagging, choking sound and Les looked between the young man and the one rolling around on the floor in agony. When he tried to lock eyes with Michael again to ask him a question, the young man was walking away.

"Hey, where are you going?" Les called.

"To make more friends," Michael said with gritted teeth.

He knew where he was going, and the big man's smile was the brightest thing he could see in the barracks. King held out one huge hand when Michael got close and Michael took it. King shook hands with him, his large mitt totally engulfing Michael's.

"You never let a snake like Jeff get away with something like that. Law of the jungle. You gotta put them down hard. Otherwise they won't respect you. Respect and power is how you going to survive in here." King told Michael.

"He liked my shoes," Michael replied.

King threw his head back and laughed, "Yes son, that I think he did."

"Thank you, King," Michael said, not knowing if he should use 'Mister' in front of King, or if that was his first name or last name...

"No problem. He had something shiny I wanted," he flashed Michael a smile, "besides, if you really want to thank me, get me some stuff at the cafeteria during breakfast and dinner this week and we'll call it even."

THE WORLD BLEEDS

"Sure, what do you want?" Michael asked, feeling relieved.

"Juice, sugar packets… but you have to get the coffee otherwise they won't give out sugar packets and tomatoes."

Michael burned that into memory and nodded.

"When do we eat?" He asked.

"That's the fun part, you have to get a job and do your work or you won't." King's smile was radiant.

"Alrighty then, and after that I need to escape this joint," Michael said softly, mostly to himself.

"You and me both kid, you and me both." King's voice rang deep within Michael's soul.

CHAPTER 7

Choccolocco, Alabama

Henry, did you…?" John's words trailed off as Henrikas came into sight.

He had two backpacks and the M2 slung over his shoulder, and he tossed it all at John's feet.

"That is what I was able to save before they searched the area too much. They found your pistol in the car when they were searching."

"How did you find this? Why didn't they take it?" John asked.

"You were unconscious for a time. I slipped down when they weren't looking and retrieved the rifle. I was able to get the backpacks after they left. They never even bothered looking in them."

"This is amazing, thank you!" John took the rifle and worked the bolt, before field stripping and inspecting it.

"That is an old gun, is it any good?"

"It served America through many wars," John said with a grin.

"I meant, does it still operate? I do not have any ammunition left for my weapon."

John nodded as he slid everything back together. He dug through Michael's pack and then the other. "You didn't find any magazines for this, did you?" he asked, his heart sinking.

"No, just the one inside the rifle. It's thirty rounds, yes?"

"Yeah, I just hope it's enough."

§ § §

"No one is here," Henrikas said, walking through the ruins of John's house.

"Yeah. I'm worried about checking their house."

"We can only try, my friend." Henrikas told him.

The two of them moved efficiently and quietly to Michael's house. If anything, it looked like it had been gone through worse, judging by the clothing scattered across the garage floor. John slowed down and looked through things, trying to make sense, trying to find a pattern. After a few minutes of poking through debris, he went into the house and made sure they were alone before heading into Michael's room. The tornado had struck in there as well, and it was twice as bad as before. Only the area behind the door and the door's path was clear. That got John to thinking and he swung the door closed and smiled.

"What is this?" Henrikas asked.

"FCI Talladega," John mused, pulling the note off the corkboard that was on the back of the door.

John was certain that hadn't been there before and he turned it over and saw half a note scrawled in the same red ink as the front.

"*John, getting clothes and heading to FEMA camp with Command...*"

He handed the note to Henrikas and smiled.

"FCI Talladega?" Henrikas asked.

"You don't know what that is?"

"No, should I?" Henrikas asked, looking confused.

"Where was the big camp you were telling me about?"

"It was an old prison, I do not know where. I remember it was named after the forests around here."

"Federal Corrections Institute... The Talladega Federal Prison. Smart boy," John said smiling.

"You know where this is?"

"I do, but I think we need to make a phone call first."

"Phone call? I told you, I have no radio equipment." Henrikas said.

"Don't worry. In half a day, we can hike there unless we can find some bicycles. Come on."

THE WORLD BLEEDS

§ § §

HOMESTEAD, KENTUCKY

"…So for a solar oven you make some sort of box with a glass or clear top. As long as you have a way to direct the sunlight towards your cooking surface, you're good. You can easily make one out of a box, with tinfoil for reflectors, clear Saran Wrap and a dark colored pot. Most of you have some sort of solar oven already and don't even know it, and you can use it to dry out foods and make jerky." Blake took his hand off the transmitter so he could get a drink of water.

"What's that? Over," a voice said into the headset.

"Your car. Don't you ever notice how hot it gets if you leave your car in the sun with all the windows up? Over." Blake loved the feel of Sandra's hand working on the knots in his shoulder.

"Ooooooohhhhhhh. That's a great idea… er… over," a tiny voice that definitely belonged to an adolescent said.

"Hey, I don't recognize your voice little man, what's your name? Over?" Blake said getting into it.

"Jeremiah sir, I just found out about this frequency this past week and have been listening in. It's really helped. Uh… Over."

"Well, feel free to call me anytime. Your parents too. Over."

"My parents got taken by the soldiers, over."

Sandra stiffened, but started to work on the muscles above the gunshot that had healed nicely, but had left the spot of the wound sore and the muscles taut.

"Oh? Where are you at? Over."

"I'm in Arkansas, near Texarkana. Over."

"I'm sorry to hear that son," a new voice broke in and both Blake and Sandra froze in shock. They hadn't heard that voice since the day Kenny had taken Sandra at knifepoint. "Maybe we can work on getting this country back from the foreigners. Over."

Sandra grabbed the mic, "Is this John the squid, over?"

A hearty chuckle answered her before he could spoke, "I thought I remembered you. Yeah, John the squid. You were the hand-to-hand instructor at Bragg if I remember correctly? Over."

"No, that was Sergeant Melissa Sandusky, an Ohio girl, but if you remember her you must be her ex, John." Sandra said.

"Oh crap, I'm sorry, I heard Sandra and figured... Wow small world. I remember you too. Over."

"Yeah, what can we help you with on Rebel Radio tonight John? Over." Sandra asked and sat down next to Blake who was giving her an odd look.

"Ghost of the past," Sandra whispered to him, waiting to hear the response.

"Mostly looking for survivors, listening and gathering Intel. I imagine the NATO forces and

THE WORLD BLEEDS

ISIS bands are trying to find you all by Direction Finding. I can go scramble but I figure you all knew this already and are set up pretty good. Am I right? Over."

"Yes, it would take a full battalion to dig us out, maybe more. We broadcast on open frequencies for this to help folks out. Over."

"Well, maybe y'all can help me. Some folks I care about got snagged and are stuck at a FEMA camp. When I heard you call this Rebel Radio I had to call… Are there any rebels in the Anniston, Alabama area you are in contact with? I'm going to change back to that frequency I first contacted you on and go to scramble, over."

"Well I'll be." Sandra stood up to let David get sit down.

Blake stood up and motioned for his wife, but she shook her head and paced.

"See if you can get him," Sandra asked before wrapping her arms around Blake's chest.

"I do already, here." David handed her the mic and turned up the volume a bit.

"Sandra here, go ahead."

"They got my son's best friend, and two little kids that were with us. Sandra, if you remember me, you know I won't let this stand. They are in a FEMA camp near Anniston."

"I do remember you, you went after those guys in Afghanistan with Melissa. I heard they pushed you out and after that you went home. To answer your question, yes, we've heard about survivors all over the country. How bad is it? Over."

"I saw three squads for sure, armor and—"

"Excuse me," a cultured European voice broke into the transmission, "You wouldn't be talking about my camp, would you?"

"Who is this?" John demanded.

"Commander Lukashenko, NATO liaison for this area of the gulf. If you'd like to be reunited with your friends, I can make those arrangements." His voice was cold and he reminded Blake of a rattlesnake; deadly and unpredictable.

"Comrade, how has the prison warden job been treating you?" Another voice broke into the transmission, but had the same sound of feedback as John.

"Henrikas, I thought… Well, now I know you are still alive. We should—"

"Next set in the lineup," Sandra interrupted before working the radio herself and changing the frequency.

They waited for long moments before they heard John's voice come on.

"I'm getting too old for this. Do you think he'll figure out what frequency we're on? Over."

"No," Sandra said, pressing the transmit button, "Not right away. Check back within four hours. Skip the next two in the lineup and radio back in. Over."

"You're going to make me do math, and I hate math. Ok, four hours, skip the next two frequencies and do the third from this one. Thanks, and please…" John's voice was strained.

"We've got a lot of reach on this base unit, and we've got some active military working with us now. They are in contact with other guys. Let us network and I'll have more info to give you a sitrep in four hours. Sound good? Over."

"Thank you. Too bad you aren't Sandusky, I was going to rib Blake some, over."

"…Out," She handed the mic back to David and stretched.

"David, can you get Sgt. Smith up here and set his communications guy loose rounding up all legitimate units stateside down by Alabama?"

"No problem. What's that stuff about next steps?" David asked.

"Oh, it's something we did. We'd take our channel or frequency and add a number to it to get the next one. It was totally random and I didn't think John would remember the one we had used all that long ago," Sandra said.

"I thought you said Sandusky was a different lady?" Blake asked, confused.

"She is. Remember when I told you I was sometimes a door gunner?" she asked, realizing her husband was feeling a touch of jealousy.

"Yeah?"

"It was to pull out John. He went UNORDER and did what he had to do."

"Un order?" Blake asked.

"Unless Otherwise Directed; he ran his own Op to get back some villagers the Taliban had kidnapped. He left a trail of bodies all the way to the pickup point. I think he had a half a magazine left and his knife was bloody."

"What's that have to do with Sandusky?" Blake asked.

"Melissa was the one flying the chopper we stole," Sandra said, her eyes twinkling mischievously.

"You stole… Duncan!" Blake mock yelled and Sandra laughed, giving him a kiss.

"Do you really think we can help him?" Blake asked as they headed arm in arm towards the front porch.

"Yes, I truly think we can. At least with information. Rebel radio, it really… really is a Rebel Radio station…"

CHAPTER 8

TALLADEGA FEDERAL PENITENTIARY &
TEMPORARY FEMA CAMP, ALABAMA

I t wasn't an hour into Michael's new 'job' and his hands already ached. The work itself wasn't difficult, but it was mind numbingly boring . He was winding copper wire by hand onto electrical motors. There were literally truckloads of materials for them to put together. There was a trained 'supervisor' every twenty feet of work table to make sure everyone was doing it right. He was cordial enough to Michael at first, but became increasingly belligerent as he urged Michael to work faster.

"My hands hurt," he mumbled when the supervisor had vented his spleen.

"It is your patriotic duty to do your own part. Camps around the country are—" The man spit, and he had an almost Germanic sounding accent.

"I don't even want to be here, now you are

telling me I have to work to eat… I'm ok with that, but why not let us go and do our own thing—"

Michael's body shook as the taser darts hit his back. He fell off the bench he was sitting on and writhed on the floor until the guard that had come up behind him was satisfied. He pulled the wires out and reloaded the device and looked around.

"There will be no talk of this. You all should be so happy to have a safe place to live, and food to eat," Commander Lukashenko said, approaching the commotion, "Ah, my friend Michael. This is most unfortunate. Yosef, why was he disciplined?"

"He was not fast enough and when I corrected him, he talked about leaving. We were told to not allow—"

"Yes, yes. Michael?" the Commander held out his hand and helped Michael to his feet, only to see him flop on the bench facing the guards.

"Yes sir?" Michael's voice was quivering, his nerve endings still feeling like sparks were shooting through his body.

"We cannot have that sort of treasonous talk. You are new here so you aren't aware of it… Your country suffered an attack upon its infrastructure and an orderly rebuilding process is necessary to preserve your culture."

"Commander, I don't mind working. I've always understood an honest day's pay for an honest day's work, but my hands are killing me. Is it possible for me to do another job?" Michael held up his hands to show how quickly the blisters had formed.

THE WORLD BLEEDS

"Why was he issued no gloves?" Lukashenko asked Yosef.

"We do not have any at this moment." Yosef said.

"Resupply was supposed to come in today, has it not all been checked in?"

Michael listened to them chatter and realized that the Commander had been away from the facility for a time and neither of them had a chance to catch up. Michael was largely forgotten and wondered if he should wait, or return to work...

Somebody tapped him on the shoulder and he turned to see Les across from him. He showed him his palms that had three inches of duct tape across them. Michael showed him his ruined hands, the blisters covering that area. Les winced and shook his head.

"Ok, so regarding the problem of the new kid here?" Yosef asked.

Lukashenko turned to Michael. "You will work with me, your hands are a mess. Yosef, I shall return him in a few days after his hands have healed."

"Yes sir," Yosef snapped to attention and saluted.

It was a salute that Michael wasn't familiar with, but he recognized it for what it was. The Commander was one of the big dogs in this place and ran more than a couple military APCs around the countryside kidnapping survivors. He was in charge of a forced labor camp.

"Have you eaten yet?" Lukashenko asked.

"No sir," Michael said softly, standing to join the

Commander.

"Come with me, we shall get something to eat and you can tell me about your eye. It looks like you've already had a difficult time here."

"You aren't kidding," Michael mumbled, but it was heard and Lukashenko laughed and clapped him on the shoulder and smiled.

"A fighting spirit. That is good."

§ § §

Lunch was strained and Michael got strange looks from survivors who saw him sitting with the Commander and his lieutenants. The NATO soldiers were looking at him funny because they were probably curious as to why a boy had the right hand seat next to the Commander. Michael just kept eating and remembered the promise he'd made to King earlier, so he filled his tray with the items the other man had wanted. The conversation at the table was halted and strained until somebody asked a question in a different language. Michael's look of confusion was all they needed and the table talked again. That went on for a while until a lull in the conversation had Michael looking up to see everyone staring at him.

"…And this American boy," Lukashenko said in English, "is a perfect example. He was struck in the face, bruised his knuckles defending himself, and tore his hands up knowing he did not have proper gear. Then Yosef tased him before the boy knew the rules. He stood up and talked to us with respect, when he has every reason to despise us. I think he'd be perfect to help us explain things before we have more… unpleasantness, like last week?"

"What do you have in mind, Commander?" one of the officers asked, and Michael noticed the subtle differences in the uniforms now.

"His hands are no good for wiring, I suppose we could ship him off to a different camp, but what if I allowed him to work with me on some projects while he heals and let him talk to whoever he talks to? You," Lukashenko pointed to a different officer, "say he was seen with Les and King. They are our biggest troublemakers, but the boy already has at least their respect if not friendship. Is this crazy idea?" His English was good, but in some spots he struggled to find the right words.

There was a pregnant silence at the table for a while, and then an officer two seats to Michael's right spoke up, "As long as he isn't in the long term planning meetings, I see no flaws to the plan, Commander."

"Da, yes, ya," the rest of the table chorused.

"Do you want to work with me?" Lukashenko looked at Michael over his right shoulder.

"Yes sir, I do sir. Can I ask a question?"

"Yes, by all means," Lukashenko answered.

"You want me to report back to the others? They'll think you're planting misinformation, won't they?"

The table went silent and then everyone

including the Commander began to laugh.

"Yes, that isn't something I thought of, but now that you mention it... That is a valid concern, one I had not thought of. See, this American boy will be the perfect... how do you say it... the go-between? Translator? So we can make the folks here understand."

There were nods at the table and genuine smiles of relief. Michael went with it because he didn't understand their relief, but as long as they weren't making the evil eye or sharpening a spoon to use on him, he'd do it. His hands were starting to throb worse, and he hoped that working for the Commander wouldn't put too much distance between himself and the rest.

"Ahhh, some snacks to return to the bunks?" Lukashenko asked Michael quietly.

Michael looked at the handful of sugar packets and the unopened juice box, "Uh... yeah."

"Here, take mine," Lukashenko pulled a handful of sugar packets out of his pocket and slid them into Michael's hand under the table, "Gulag wine is an acquired taste. You surprise me, truly you do. Bring me some."

"I don't know what they're going to do with it, I was just told that these were valuable for trade," Michael whispered without moving his head.

"Good. Whoever told you that has your best interests at heart. Don't be obvious, but you should be able to get some from time to time."

"Yes sir."

THE WORLD BLEEDS

§ § §

Michael had just gotten back inside the men's barracks when Les stepped out, leaning in a doorway. He stepped in front of Michael to slow him.

"Hey," Michael said.

"So, special assistant to the big dog. You have to suck a lot of…" Les's words were cut off when a big brown hand grabbed his shirt front and pulled him off his feet.

Les's butt hit the floor at the same time as Michael moved to stop King from hurting the downed man.

"Hey, King… I got what we talked about. Les," He held his hand out and helped the man to his feet, "You're right. The Commander has me working with him. I'll tell you all about it, maybe you can help me make sense of things?"

King gave Michael a look and then walked to the row of cells. Les looked at Michael with anger.

"You got what he talked about?"

"Yeah, he asked me to grab some stuff from the cafeteria for helping me earlier," Michael told him and Les's face relaxed.

"Oh, I thought it was something worse… weapons like a knife or…"

"What is it with you two? I got the impression that you're in charge of the men's dorms but King—"

"King's got his own thing going," Les answered before Michael could point out that nobody including Les messed with the big man.

"Ok. Let me drop my stuff off to King and I'll fill you in. It's really weird." Michael's voice was excited, but he winced in pain when he put his hand in his pocket.

"Ok, hurry back."

By King's cell he saw Jeff, but he slinked away before Michael got close. There were two men outside King's open cell door, but they saw the bandaged hands and looked Michael in the eyes before stepping aside and allowing him in.

"King, I got—"

"Kid, are we going to have a problem with the Commander?" King was abrupt, his brow furrowed.

"No, no. In fact, he said this stuff was for Gulag wine or something?" Michael pulled out a pocketful of sugar packets and two juice boxes.

One of the men in the doorway whistled and King gave him a sharp look that silenced him.

"How did you smuggle all of this out?"

"I… I didn't. I just… Lukashenko gave me his, he had a pocketful too."

King pondered that for a second, until the furrowed brow eased into an easy smile.

"I think he was trying to get on your good side. Is he having you be the prison liaison or something?"

"Yeah, but I got the impression that he was trying to be sincere." Michael said, sitting on the end of the cot that King had pointed at.

"Let me see your hands," King said, no question in his tone.

THE WORLD BLEEDS

Michael showed him. King unwrapped them slowly, "The officer's medic did this?"

"Yes," Michael told the big man.

"Good, maybe they are being sincere. Lord knows we have them outnumbered."

The look of relief on Lukashenko's face... the thought was like a jolt of lightening. He explained it to King who smiled and they talked for a while, forgetting about the contraband they had left out in the open.

CHAPTER 9

THE HOMESTEAD, KENTUCKY

S gt. Smith, do we have everything set?" Sandra asked as the core group had dinner together on Blake's porch, with many of the other residents sitting in the grass around them.

"Yes, ma'am. We have about a battalion's worth of '*Rebel*' units in the gulf area. I've put that Seal in contact with the closest group. They've been organizing quietly, ready to start pushing back. It was much worse than we thought. I'm sorry we didn't know—"

"I didn't know," Blake said, "and I've been married to that radio as much as David and Patty lately," placating him.

Chris smiled and pulled on his Dad's arm, vying for attention. He pulled his son close with his bad arm, feeling the stiff muscles work.

THE WORLD BLEEDS

"What do we do now?" somebody from the crowd asked.

Blake looked around. Everyone was looking at him, and it was an uncomfortable thing to realize. He was the man who wanted to live in the hills, have a solitary life. So much had changed in just a handful of months that it blew him away… Love, change of lifestyle, family and now a small community was growing up on his ten acre homestead… Granted, he still had all the fields his grandparents had handshake agreements on, but what to do now?

"Duncan, you were the one who studied this much, much more than I did. Do you have any idea?" Blake asked.

"Well, I can tell you that I don't have enough information to tell you that. It sounds like people are starting to get organized and scrape enough parts together or," Duncan paused a moment, "acquire the radios like your young video game kid you talk to on the radio sometimes."

"What about the invasion? The notes Neal and I found…" Patty said, her voice somewhat shrill.

"I don't know. But if NATO is here and our own Navy isn't, I don't know. I don't have enough information. Organize, get ready for the winter, and survive."

"No bigger picture ideas from me. When I studied this kind of stuff, they didn't have a quick and easy solution to jumpstarting the country after something like this. We always thought it'd never happen within our lifetimes. I really hope they were wrong," Duncan's words were off the cuff, but they had a chilling effect.

"You know what, this isn't so bad. My kids love it here and I'm healthier now than I was two months ago when I had a car to take me everywhere," one of the women spoke loudly from the back of the group.

There was a general murmur of agreement, but the notion that not in this lifetime… it was a hard one for many of them to swallow.

"You're all welcome to stay here, for as long as you want," Blake told them.

"If we can get your old tractor fired up, could we start laying in our own crops? Like a bigger scale?" Sandra asked.

"I don't see why not. I've always done things on a smaller scale. I could take care of a big garden… You know, there has to be full fields planted all around here, would it be safe for us—" Blake was saying but Martha interrupted him.

"You know what Blake, that's a damn good idea. I don't think enough people in our county survived the fires from the downed plane to have picked the fields clean. I bet you there's a ton of food out there." Martha said.

"Ok, so we're good for food. I'd still like to look for some livestock," Blake grumbled.

"You getting tired of squash and pork?" Sandra ribbed him.

"You know, I never thought that the end of the world would have me missing ice cream," Blake said, his words wistful. "I would have that as a treat about once a month and now it's gone... I was thinking about it and I think we could figure something out. We have to get smarter about food preservation. I don't have enough jars to can everything for everyone... Granted that last food truck had almost two pallets full."

"You worry too much," Sandra said, sitting on his knee, his good leg.

Her weight comforted him, her very presence. He put his good arm around her waist and held her close. Chris took his free hand, perhaps due to a little bit of jealousy or to remind Blake that he was still there. He had to smile and decided to listen to his wife.

"You know, I have an idea on making a cold storage room, but I don't think I can handle the construction for a while."

"You have enough volunteers who owe you one," a yell came from one of the rescued men, and several more laughed and cheered.

Blake was amazed. He knew folks were grateful, but he'd never expected that and, at that moment, he realized something that shocked him. Sandra and Duncan ran the security of The Homestead as well as Sgt. Smith who in turn organized his own men... But Blake had become the figurehead of the group. They looked at him expectantly.

"Ok, well, I had an idea for building a springhouse. Any of you know what those are?"

A teenage girl who was sitting with her parents

slowly snaked her hand up in the air. She'd been sitting in the grass with her mother and brother. She was one of the newer members that Sandra's squad had found walking and looking for somewhere safe.

"I'm sorry ma'am, I don't know your name or if I did the knock to the head might have scrambled me some."

"I'm Viola, Mr. Jackson. We learned about them when we were doing our history lessons," her eyes cut sideways to confirm with one of the other kids, "People would cut ice from the lakes and put it in an icehouse. The runoff would go downhill or something into a house and the cold water and evaporation kept it cooler?"

"Very good. If anybody's interested in helping, I'd like to build one of those."

"That sounds like a good idea Blake, but uh… there's no lake around here and more importantly, there's no ice," Duncan said, his expression betraying the fact that he thought Blake might be a little scrambled after all.

"No, but we have cold runoff already. The artesian well that runs through the Barracks. We make a different place for the bathrooms down there and then…"

"None of us use the bathroom there Blake," Bobby said, "No privacy, although some of us have dunked our heads in the water a time or two. That water's cold!"

Blake thought about that a moment. It raised the question on where they *were* going to the bathroom, but didn't voice it. He figured Martha had sorted that one out, but he made a mental note to ask her later on.

"Well, I guess we need to figure out where the water comes out of the barn, then pick a spot for the springhouse. We'll dig a spot out, line the bottom with plastic or clay and fill with a bunch of gravel. The water's natural evaporation and temperature will keep the temps down. It'll be like a fridge if we can insulate the side."

"The side?" Duncan asked him.

"Well, I was thinking about digging into the hillside, a good ways actually, and have it earth sheltered," Blake told him.

"How is that different than the big room in the bottom of the barn, Daddy?" Chris asked from his side.

Sandra got up to walk around and Blake smiled, in truth his leg had started to get pins and needles. Blake stood as well and gripped the railing. His shoulder and arm still hurt and his leg throbbed, but not even half as bad as it had a week ago. He was healing, and healing fast.

"That artesian well must be deep if it's colder than the air in the barracks. The barracks will stay 55 all year as deep as it is, without a heat source. I figure that water has to be in the forties. Almost as cold as a refrigerator. If we earth shelter it and put a good side on it with an insulated door, we might even be able to make and store our own ice inside of it for the coming months next spring. Maybe we'd even be able to make ice cream at that point," Blake smiled at his own joke.

"Good thing then," Sandra said, running her hands across Blake's stubble, "because I'll be dying for ice cream and pickle sandwiches soon." She gave him the biggest smile and walked over and picked Chris up.

Realization slapped Blake square in the face and his jaw dropped open.

"Are you sure?"

"Yup," Sandra said smiling.

"Does that mean I'm going to have a baby brother to play with?" Chris asked, his voice loud and clear.

The group had gone silent and the ladies present were smiling, some whispering to their husbands who just didn't get the joke until they heard Chris's question. Blake let out a surprised sound and almost crushed the two of them in a bear hug, ignoring the pain in his shoulder. The Homestead erupted in cheers and polite clapping. Blake didn't hear any of it, he was too lost in his wife's eyes.

"I was scared you would be upset," Sandra whispered to him.

"No, never," Blake told her.

"You're squishing my guts out," Chris told them theatrically and then blew a raspberry at them when Sandra put him down.

"You better watch that, your face might freeze like that," Duncan said and they all cracked up again.

THE WORLD BLEEDS

§ § §

The construction of the spring house started almost immediately, with most of the idle hands available helping out. They dug down the side wall of the barn until they found where an earthen pipe came out. It was quite deep, and they considered trenching all of it out, until somebody pointed out they still had to dig out the foundation of the spring house itself. They decided to start digging every twenty feet down the hill until they came to a spot that was perfect for what they wanted to do, and was situated enough away from the toe poppers that the kids wouldn't be a problem. They started to dig with shovels and picks, Blake using his old tractor and the back blade to scrape it out as much as he could. The spring house ended up being roughly twenty foot by twenty.

Curt took Blake's chainsaw and headed into the North West side of the property with one of the quads. The homestead could hear several trees coming down and the buzz of the saw, and soon they saw him driving slowly, a tow rope dragging the main trunk of a pine tree. He'd already trimmed it and the nubs where the limbs had been were digging gouges in the pasture grass. Blake nodded when he saw it and smiled. That was going to be one of the main beams, and he began explaining how to build and brace it. It took many trips to get enough wood and Blake had Duncan sat down to discuss the one part they had overlooked. The gravel.

BOYD CRAVEN

"You know, there are coal mines all over this state. What are the chances we can find something already loaded and use the old semi we found?

"Hm…" Blake mused, "I don't know honestly. We can always do it a little bit at a time… we have what's left of summer."

"We'll figure something out," Duncan said.

"You always do," Sandra's voice cut through the reverie. "That kiddo is on the radio and asking for you," Sandra told him.

Blake stood, making sure his cane was handy, and walked up the hill slowly.

"You ok there, old man?" Sandra poked him in the side, making him jump.

"Yeah, just stiff from sitting. I'm glad we're doing this, we really needed something like this and—"

"And some of them needed the work. Idle hands and all of that," Sandra finished the thought for him.

Blake gave his wife a quick kiss, "Why do I even bother talking if you already know what I'm going to say?"

"Exactly!" Sandra poked him again and ran up the hill.

Blake smiled. For such a dangerous warrior, there was still more than a little bit of the carefree girl left in his wife. Even the grid going down and the subsequent danger hadn't taken that away from her, and Blake's heart swelled. Chris ran down the hill where he had been playing with some kids to shadow Blake on the way back up.

THE WORLD BLEEDS

"Hey, Dad, your house thing almost done?" Chris asked.

"Getting there. What are you up to?"

"Some of the rabbits had babies. They're everywhere! And the chickens are sitting on some eggs now and…"

"Things are getting busy here, aren't they?" Blake asked.

"Yeah! Isn't it really neat?"

"It sort of is little buddy, it sort of is."

§ § §

"Z, this is Blake, how you doing kiddo?"

An exaggerated sigh came out of the radio and David laughed into his hand when she answered, "I'm good. I need a way to recharge these batteries for this unit and I tried the trick of that AC DC converter with car batteries and it doesn't work, over."

"Oh… that's because the circuit in the AC/DC converter is probably fried. Let me think a minute," Blake said. "What kind of batteries are they? Over," Blake asked her.

She told him and it didn't do much for his understanding. "I don't know—"

"Excuse me Blake, I may have a solution," a voice cut in. Not one he recognized.

"Sure, by all means," Blake said looking to see that they were on an open frequency.

"Miss, I was listening the day you found that

radio. If you go back to where you found it, there's a bound to be a charger. Your unit has a USB plug on it, yes?" The voice was cultured and without any discernible accent.

"Yes?" Z answered.

"Ah good, it works much like your American's smart phones. It has a box where you can plug in a battery pack or plug the cord into the side of the unit. They are EMP shielded, so they should work here. A cigarette lighter male adapter is what they use. You can rig up a female adapter to any 12v source and charge it that way. There are more 12v sources than you can imagine," the voice replied.

They were all silent a moment, considering the message as much as how it was delivered. It wasn't lost on Blake that the stranger had said 'your American's smart phones', and the wording.

"Where are you from, Comrade?" Blake asked, taking a shot in the dark, knowing many Russian Block countries had made up much of the Southern seaboard from transmissions coming out of Georgia, Alabama and south Florida.

"Georgia, over." The voice sounded amused.

"Country or state?" Patty asked Blake.

"Does it really matter?" Blake asked.

Z spoke up. "Hey, I think I remember seeing a box like that. It had these big clips on one end like a battery charger has, thanks! Over."

"She didn't need me after all," Blake told Sandra smiling.

"No, but maybe everyone can start pulling

together to help, even if it's over the radio. What was your take on the guy from 'Georgia'," she asked, making air quotes with her fingers.

"He knows a lot about the hardware she's talking about. Do you think it's a defector or…?"

"Hard to say," said Sandra. "From what we've heard from John, there have been defections, but they are at risk just as much, or more, from the big camps. I guess we're too far out in the country for them to worry about us… Do you think we should reach out to folks like them? They should have some good intel."

"You're more the expert than I am, why are you asking me?" Blake poked at his wife with a finger grinning as she dodged out of the way.

"You might not have the same experience, but you are the kind of guy who looks at a broken part and figures out how to fix it or build it up better, even if you don't have the right tools or equipment. It's guys like you—" she broke off and wiped her eyes.

"Don't cry mommy," Chris said, wrapping his arms around her waist.

"I just… I'm sorry. It's too early for me to claim hormones, so maybe the whole thought of Chris and the baby growing up in this is getting me down. That talk Dad had earlier… where they never expected things to get better—"

"Guys like me need women like you, to hold us up and keep us strong. I've learned so much from you. It's why I'm not worried or sad about this. Together we can do anything. Even survive a zombie apocalypse."

"Zombies?" Chris almost shouted, startling everyone.

"No no, I didn't really mean zombies, Chris. I meant—"

"Brains…." Chris started to stagger around the room dragging a foot, holding his arms out.

Everyone cracked up at that and Lisa walked in the room to catch the end of his theatrics. Lisa rolled her eyes and hooked a finger in Patty's direction. Patty got up and headed towards the kitchen.

"Where'd you learn that?" Blake asked, still chuckling.

"Cartoons. Everybody knows zombies eat your brains," Chris told Blake earnestly.

"Zombies are pretend. They aren't real, Hon." Sandra told him.

"Are zombies really pretend?" Chris asked David, hoping for a friendly answer.

"Naw, they're pretend… but if they were real, your mom and dad here would be master zombie slayers." David said deadpan and smiled when Chris busted up in giggles.

"Ok, really though," Blake said, his tone changing, "About the defectors… They are people too. I'm sure they came here to get a better life, just like every one of our ancestors did."

Sandra thought about that a moment, biting her lip, and then she nodded.

"Ok, let's keep an ear out for them. I don't want

us or anyone listening out there suckered into a trap."

"Yeah, but I don't see how that's any more dangerous than everything else that's gone on out there." Blake told her.

"Very true, you never know who you can trust," Patty said, walking back into the room with Lisa, a grin on her face.

CHAPTER 10

TALLADEGA FCI

I hope that you weren't harmed," the Commander was telling Michael as they sat together at lunch time.

"No, no sir. It was just a small disagreement. I liked my shoes much better than the prisoner," Michael told him, leaving out King's involvement and the shank.

"This is why people think we are using them as forced labor. If we could be resupplied more often, then supplies such as gloves, shoes and sanitary supplies would go a long way towards making conditions easier, I think."

"Probably, sir. Just by my bunk alone, half a dozen men have no shoes, and they wash their jumpsuits in the sinks on their days off and walk around in their boxers, and then wash those when

THE WORLD BLEEDS

the jumpsuits are dry." Michael told him after pausing to consider his phrasing.

"Do you or the people who you are talking to know of a solution of this? Your country's infrastructure is what's truly making this difficult… for example, the materials are out there within this country. The problems are arising from the general lawlessness that's been happening as of late and the difficulties in identifying where such things are kept," the Commander told him, then held up a finger as his radio squawked.

While Commander Lukashenko spoke to one of his officers in a foreign language, Michael took a moment to consider what he was going to say next. He'd been spending the past few days shadowing the Commander, getting an understanding for what was going on. Yesterday for a time, he was even able to spend some time with Linny and Bret when the kids' dorms allowed them all to come out and play. He'd asked them how they were being treated and what they had been up to. Of all the answers that they could have given, he was surprised by what they told him.

There was plenty of food and clothing and, although they had to do their 'schoolwork', they were generally happy. The kids were dormed in three areas of the old office building. The main conference rooms were full of bunks for kids twelve and under and the office spaces were emptied out and crammed with beds for boys and girls over that age up to seventeen years. Then the kids went to the adult side, like Michael had. He'd asked them about guards and the kids had told Michael that the teachers and hall monitors were all they had. They didn't carry guns in there, except for the guys by the door. Michael tucked that information away for later.

They spent the rest of the time joking about how bad the food was, but it was Bret who said he'd rather go back to eating stinky fish than the soggy vegetables that they made the kids eat. The only thing about the visit that had gotten ugly was when a man who was visiting with his kids had gotten hysterical about seeing his wife. An unsympathetic guard had whispered something to him and he'd gone off and had started to swing his fists before being brought down by three guards and the use of a taser. That had piqued Michael's interest, because he hadn't heard about the women being able to visit and mingle with their families much. As a matter of fact, most of the grumbling he'd heard had made him feel sick.

The rumor was that the guards were keeping the women away from the men for their own 'use'. It had caused a lot of resentment and more than a few ill-formulated plans of revenge from the men, but it was all mutterings. Many of the people in his barracks were broken of spirit and had given up. Michael thought it was quite sad to see so many broken souls gathered in one place. It hadn't been that long ago that everything had worked, and now many of them worked listlessly while their hearts and minds were in other places.

"Yes, yes. Da." Lukashenko said, putting his radio down and turned to find Michael deep in thought.

"Michael, so do you see the problems we are having here? It isn't like it's a forced labor camp. Parts to rebuild the power structure must be manufactured. There are only a few places in the world to build the equipment and motors needed to build a new power plant, or the parts to fix the transformers. Then there's the problem of all of the airplanes that fell, causing untold death and destruction. Much worse than your country's 9/11."

"Huh?" Michael asked, his attention snapping back to the Commander, "Oh, yes, yes sir. I can't imagine what it's like with the rest of the country. I remember hearing or reading somewhere that there were over five thousand planes flying at any given moment over the country."

"Exactly. So this camp is producing electrical motors, and another facility is hand placing and soldering parts to rebuild circuit boards, and another facility is replacing parts in a SMT line at an electronics factory using parts we were able to bring with us from our home countries."

"Sir, what's an SMT line and if it isn't uh… secret, but where is everyone from? Your men from NATO that is." Michael asked, hoping his questions weren't too probing.

"Ahhh, SMT means surface mount technology. They have these amazing machines that can make circuit boards in a matter of minutes, whereas hand placing parts would take days and days. It's for rebuilding the components. If your countrymen can keep this rate up, we should be able to start restoring power to areas in as little as two years. As to your second question, yes, we are from all over. My unit is mostly from Eastern European countries."

"Russia?"

"Some countries were once part of Russia, yes."

"Thank you sir. I do have one more question, and it's somewhat related to the man who had to be... disciplined. The men are more than a little curious..."

"Ahhh, would you be asking about the women?"

"Yes sir, there are rumors—" Michael started to say.

"Rumors? What are these?"

"That the women are kept separate for... sex. That your men keep the women for themselves," Michael's face burned, but not with embarrassment or shame like the Commander thought, but in anger.

"Ahhh, that is what they think? Sex is part of it, but not what you think at all."

Michael's eyes locked with the Commander's, and he gave Lukashenko a questioning look.

"We do not have a large medical staff with supplies. If the women became pregnant, it would only take a handful of them doing so to tax us beyond our capacity. As it is, we are having a hard time getting supplies for the ladies who came to us already pregnant. Is this truly a sticking point with the men?"

"Yes sir, it really is. A lot of folks feel like they have been imprisoned and forced to work while being separated by their families. There isn't a lot of love for you and your men here. A lot of folks think they'd rather try the outside on their own, but that isn't allowed—"

"You are correct Michael, it isn't allowed. Maybe it's the difference in our cultures that make this so hard for each side to understand. On one side, we are here to protect you, and we are here in America to help you rebuild your country. Many of us are away from our homes and families, and some countries' soldiers are conscripted or... drafted? So we cannot understand why it is that your people don't understand the sacrifice we are making to help you," Lukashenko paused and took a sip of water before going on.

"Then there is your side. You won your independence by throwing off the shackles of the British Empire, and became one of the biggest super powers the world has ever known. You want your freedom, you want your guns," Lukashenko almost spat, contempt in his voice, "and you don't want any help even though you obviously need it."

"My history lessons in school told us that America won our independence by fighting England over tyranny and taxes. We were being oppressed and pushed and didn't have any individual freedoms," Michael said.

"So, what is the point of that? That is essentially what I said," Lukashenko looked at him in disgust.

"The point is, maybe people feel like you and your men locking us up feels like the British oppression," Michael said and the look dropped off of the Commander's face and was replaced by one of shock and anger.

"They say this? They think we are the oppressors? Are you saying they are going to revolt and have their own 'civil war'?" The Commander said, using his fingers for air quotes, spittle flying from his mouth.

"No, no sir. I'm sorry for alarming you. I was just trying to help you understand our side, our culture. I thought that's what you wanted from me, an exchange of ideas and—"

"Yes. Yes, I suppose I can understand that point of view now," Lukashenko stood and turned away, his back to Michael as he looked out of the window.

Michael waited for him to continue and cringed inwardly. Talking about breaking out was a common topic, but it was done in a wistful, wishing manner rather than anything serious.

"I suppose there are many things to consider here; I'll have Yosef take you back to the barracks after the staff meeting. I must ask you to wait for me until then, as I have an idea I need to run by the long term planning committee. I cannot make this idea happen on my own."

"Idea, sir? I don't understand." Michael asked

confused by the sudden shift in tone.

"Oh, sorry. I did not mean to confuse you. I'm taking your views on the women and the rumors to heart. I need to talk to my men some and then perhaps I can form a plan to keep everyone happy. I am a family man myself. I honestly do not know what I would do if I were in your shoes. Though I am the Commander of this facility, I am merely a soldier and I have a boss I must report to as well."

"Yes sir. I understand that completely." *No, no I don't, you don't realize that you are more than just a soldier, you are our jailer*, Michael wanted to say, but he remained silent.

"Very well then. We have a planning meeting, if you could wait outside," Lukashenko said, "and I'll have Yosef take you back when we're done here. Thank you for your insight today."

§ § §

"You told him what?" Les shouted in Michael's face as he was recounting the day's events to the men who kept their barracks in check.

King was on the fringes, and staring intently at Les who had started to get incrementally more red in the face the longer the conversation had flowed, until he had finally erupted. King had begun to move, but stopped when Michael shook his head almost imperceptibly.

"I told him why people didn't like to be locked up and made to work. We were talking about the cultural differences and—"

"You are going to make him think we're trying to break out of here!" Les shouted again.

"Les, calm down man. Back off," Michael tried to take a step back, but the press of bodies was completely surrounding him, and he stepped on somebody's shoes.

"No, you could jeopardize all of this. We didn't elect you to be the liaison and you suddenly are speaking for all of us? What if we're punished or things get worse because…"

"Back off the kid," King intoned.

"Or what? Are you going to tune me up like the others? This kid comes in here and he doesn't play the game like the rest of us. I'm getting sick of worrying he'll say something that'll get us all in worse trouble than we're already in." Les shouted, unaware that Jeff had walked up behind him, nodding his head.

"I for one didn't vote for the kid to be my voice," Jeff said over Les's shoulder.

Les turned, surprised, and then turned back to stare down at Michael.

"I didn't think that sharing 'American' culture with them would hurt us, rather—" Michael's words were cut off by a vicious backhand by Les.

Michael wiped the side of his face and a crimson smear covered the back of his hand from a split lip. King pushed his way through the circle of men that had Les and him crowded in, but Michael shook his head again. The big man looked at him puzzled as

THE WORLD BLEEDS

Jeff came forward to stand at Les's side, both men had clenched fists.

"Respect and power," Michael called to King and then moved his feet into a more relaxed look, but ready to move fast if needed.

"What are you talking about?" Les asked, looking over his shoulder.

"Back off Les, guys, let me out." Michael said to the group.

When no one moved, Michael sighed. The two men took a step forward. Michael knew there was only one way out now, and although he'd never fought a grown man, he'd fought plenty of guys his age. Part of the reason he hadn't gotten in as much trouble when he got caught with the chief's daughter was that he generally went out of his way to stay out of trouble. Michael had been booted from school from time to time for fighting, but he tried to keep that out of school. It was usually a new kid looking to make a name for himself, or an argument over a girl somewhere. The fact that he avoided things like that, and was a generally nice guy with a little bit of a temper, had kept him from serious trouble.

Until now.

"No Michael, I think that you've gotten too big for your britches," Les told him, starting to circle around to Michael's side.

"I for one, would love to teach you a lesson in humility," Jeff said, coming straight for Michael.

Half a heartbeat, a deep breath and the world around the circle of bodies went silent as Michael's vision narrowed and he focused on the wild punch Jeff started to throw. He moved to his right, away from Les, dodging the haymaker. Michael landed two quick blows to the malnourished man's gut and backed to the side where the press of bodies prevented him from moving. Jeff held onto his stomach and leaned over to catch his breath. Les pushed Jeff out of the way and rushed Michael, forgoing the pretense of an orderly fight.

When Les's outstretched hands were within reach, Michael ducked his head to the side and lunged forward, using his shoulder to impact with the older man's chest. When he didn't fly back as expected and wrapped his arms around Michael's chest to start squeezing him in a bear hug, Michael tried to pull back. Les tried to throw and twist Michael to the ground but got his nose smashed when Michael whipped his head up, hitting him soundly.

The impact was enough to make Les let him go. Michael get a few steps back to look just as Jeff rushed him. Michael threw two quick rabbit punches that had no effect as Jeff turned his head away and landed his own blow to Michael's stomach. The blow pained Michael, but it didn't slow him down. Michael got a solid right cross into Jeff's chin. He started to slump, but was pushed aside again as Les tried to maneuver for position.

Instead of trying to rush the young man like he'd tried before, he swung wildly. Michael was able to easily dodge the over-projected punch and realized that he'd been dealing with an amateur. Les was bigger but he was also older, and more than a little slower. He doubled over in pain when Michael's hand flicked out, thumping him in the jewels. The move looked like a tap and it probably was, but it was expertly applied and, as Les fought down his nausea, he didn't see the knee that snapped his head back and dropped him into unconsciousness.

Michael stepped away from the side of the circle and looked at Jeff who was regaining his feet again. Apparently Jeff hadn't learned his lesson the first two times from Michael and was going for a third time. A kick to his hip sent him stumbling, returning him to his back, and a sharp stomp to his ribcage ended the fight. Neither of the men was seriously hurt, which was what Michael intended.

In his head, he had thought the fight to be necessary for two reasons. The crowd may have agreed with Les's sentiment, but if he wasn't careful he might end up with a whole barracks full of mob mentality, with him in their crosshairs. The second reason was pure survival. If he caved in or backed away, nobody would ever respect him. Michael didn't want this fight, but his blood and adrenaline were pumping from the violence. Almost stunned by his victory, he looked at the two men, watching them as the circle of men started to break up and drift away.

"Respect and power," King mumbled before he drifted into the crowd, his head seen easily over the heads of other men.

"Come on Les," Michael grumbled, nudging the man.

Les let out a low moan and opened one eye and sat up. His face was crimson from the nose down, and one of his eyes was swollen shut.

"Break it up!" somebody shouted behind Michael, and then all he knew was agony as every nerve ending in his body fired off at once in pain.

"Bring him to the Commander, he can deal with this," Michael heard, recognizing the voice of Yosef before he passed out.

CHAPTER 11

Their patrols should be coming right through here," Henrikas said, pointing to a map.

"So what we need is to get their attention, then?" a grizzled man with a Texas accent asked.

"You bet. We've got things all worked out. John and Henrikas can fill you in on the plan," a small serious man said.

"Come on Tex, let's get you squared away. Takedown is going to happen hopefully in a few hours." John told him.

John had been planning and practicing for almost a week, with a small group of operators who were able to get to his location quickly. Right away, John saw that he didn't need as many men as he had at first thought. Almost every spec. op group was represented by the dozen of them, with Tex being the last to find his way to their camp. They didn't have much time to do any more training and they filled him in on the way to the ambush site.

"Are you sure she'll do it?" Tex asked as they got into position.

"Of course she will, she's been doing stuff like this her whole life and—" John's words broke off as he got a look at the bait for their honey trap.

"She sure is purty," Tex mumbled as a stunning woman stepped into view.

Caitlin had agreed on the spot and had worked with many of the operatives before. She was retired Army and had on more than once donned revealing clothing or less to work a distraction. John had met her a day earlier but hadn't been prepared to see a cleaned up woman in an American flag style string bikini. Caitlin was all lean muscle with curves in the right places and, even in her late thirties, she turned heads hard enough to break necks. The trick of the trap though, was that she was just as good hand to hand as she was with her guns. Those she wore in thigh holsters, much like Lara Croft from Tomb Raider. The overall effect stunned the men speechless for a moment.

"Y'all ain't never seen a lady before?" Caitlin asked, her Louisiana drawl only adding to her charm.

"Not like you. Wow, you even shaved your legs," Tex said unabashedly as he took in her appearance.

"Hey, this one is cute," she told John, "Stick

around cowboy and we'll go do some fishing later on," she dropped Tex a wink and the man turned red from the roots of his hair all the way down to his neck.

"Ma'am," Tex told her after a healthy gulp and a breath of air.

The rumble of motors interrupted them and the men faded from the roadside into their positions across from Caitlin who had pulled a lounger out from somewhere. She sat in it and crossed one shapely leg over the other and grabbed a paperback book from the dried out grass underneath the chair, then lay back waiting. To anyone driving through the area, she would appear to be doing exactly what she was doing. Sunbathing. Armed with the knowledge of how women were regarded in this new world, they wanted a target. A target so tempting it would stop an APC and have its men leave the armored vehicle.

Everyone, including Caitlin, thought the plan was going to hell when the APC rolled past, but it suddenly came to a stop a hundred yards beyond her position. It reversed, swaying side to side as it backed up. There was room to turn around, and the heavier armor was up in the front, but whoever was driving was in a hurry.

John tensed as it came to a stop and the hatch opened.

"Excuse me miss, I was wondering if you could give me some directions, I appear to be lost." The man's voice was heavily accented and his words were accompanied by male laughter from within.

"Why sure, I know most places here abouts. Where y'all headed, sugar?"

"Well, we were…" he ducked his head back in and then climbed out the hatch and was followed by several men.

"Wow, there sure are a lot of ya in there. Any more of you boys want to come out and ask me for directions? Or give me some?" her words were sugar and spice and, though she didn't mean every word to drip with sexual innuendo, they did.

"Miss, my name is Lieutenant Jenkins. We're part of a NATO envoy to help folks out…" his words trailed off as Caitlin stood and stretched lazily, giving all the men a good look.

"… and we were wondering if you knew of any more survivors in the area? Directions would be helpful." Jenkins finished after a long pause.

"If there were any more people out here, why wouldn't I be with them? I've been all alone, without a man to… protect me," she batted her eyelashes.

Several men stepped forward. "I would love to be the first to offer," "Allow me Miss," "I'd be happy to…" then the lieutenant waved them all down into silence as his eyes traveled from her curves down to the twin pistols strapped to her thighs.

"Ma'am, it looks to me like you are properly… equipped," his words elicited snickers from the men and she avoided looking at the APC as one her friends dropped in silently, "but I would like to offer to take you someplace safe. We have all of

THE WORLD BLEEDS

the latest conveniences, including electricity and running water." His smile was sincere, but his eyes kept traveling up and down her body, at war with what he was seeing.

"If you can promise this girl a hot shower, I'd be happy for sure. Maybe even let you boys give me a hand or two?" she turned and walked slowly towards an abandoned house where a cooler had been set up.

Caitlin bent over and reached in the cooler with her left hand. The men who hadn't seen a woman outside of the camps in months were mesmerized momentarily and when she turned, her right hand drawing a pistol, they were caught flat-footed.

"Now, I'd offer to share this Coors with one of you fine men, but my friends are even thirstier," Caitlin said with a grin, watching the color running out of Jenkins face.

She could see their sudden panicked expressions as, like ghosts, John, Tex and the rest of the men covered the NATO soldiers and started to not so gently disarm them. They used zip ties to immobilize their hands and legs, and only one man, Lieutenant Jenkins, began resisting but John used his pistol to hammer the man into submission. Blood ran freely down his temple from a small cut, but Jenkins looked defiantly back at them.

"I think we should ask him first," Caitlin said, pulling on a button up shirt one of her team had handed her.

"I don't think so," Jenkins said with an arrogant

sniff, looking around at everyone, pissed.

"You want to poke the bear, boy?" Tex asked him.

Jenkins looked the lean Texan over and his eyes settled on the Ka-Bar. John saw the look and nodded to the lanky man.

"You know, we're covered under the Geneva Convention. Torture isn't allowed."

"Who said I was going to torture you? I'm just going to take you into the bushes and pig stick you if you don't tell me what I want to know. You'll die trying to get away. When your compadres here," Tex motioned to the rest of the men who were now on their stomachs with him, "hear your death rattle, why, I bet they'll be more than willing to give up the information we want. Won't you boys?"

A sullen silence followed.

"You going to talk?" Tex asked.

"No, you can go to hell," Jenkins said, before spitting at Tex's feet.

"Now those were my favorite boots. I really wish you wouldn't a done that. I might have played the game a little bit longer, and now you ain't going to like how this ends up."

Jenkins eyes went wide and he was about to speak, but his words were cut off when he was grabbed by the wrists and ankles where he was zip tied. All he could manage was a groan as the odd angle made it hard to breathe, let alone speak. John watched as the surprisingly strong man dragged the Lieutenant into the tall grass, about twenty yards

THE WORLD BLEEDS

away.

"Boys, y'all gonna want to listen in real good, we aren't playin' around," Caitlin told them.

They were stone faced and stared at John and the other men's boots as the 'Rebels' held them at gunpoint. Shrill screams started and a high pitch voice begged, right before one long note of agony held for almost ten seconds before abruptly cutting off with a gurgle. First one man looked left and right, his chin dragging in the dirt to see the looks of horror on his fellow soldiers faces.

"This one," Caitlin kicked the shoulder of a man who had been the second out of the APC.

John hauled him to his feet, the old grease gun nestled in the hollow spot at the top of his neck, pressing the bottom of his skull. The man winced when John turned the barrel with his right hand, his left holding his arms behind his back, putting pressure on his bound form.

"You want to have a chit chat, or do you want to…" John's words trailed off as they all watched Tex come out of the tall grass, wiping his knife with a bandanna, "or do you want me to have Tex take care of things?"

"Depends. I have friends in the area, I don't want to see them dead," the NATO soldier said.

"Sir, no," a muffled voice came from a prone figure on the end.

"Shut up," John's man said from the side of his mouth.

"Actually, that sounds fair," Caitlin said before

pulling a knife of her own and playing with the tip.

The solder watched, more interested in how the light glinted off the steel and traveled from her neck to the swell of her chest, her shirt still half buttoned. He was struggling to swallow both his fear and his lust, but when Caitlin stepped into his personal space, he caught the scent of the woman and tried to look her in the eyes. She was tall, as tall as he was, but he could see the knife she held beside his face as well, and all stray thoughts vanished.

"I know where the FEMA camp is, what I don't know, is how many more armored units are in the area and how close reinforcements are," she told him, making the reflected light from the blades edge pain his face with a warm glow.

"There's one more, and no. We can't even get supplies most of the time—"

"Sir!" The muffled voice on the end yelled, and the rebel holding him pulled him to his feet.

"Don't tell them nothing sir, they'll hang us for treason!"

"Easy there son," John said, "You and your team here mean nothing to us. As far as we're concerned, y'all are invaders. We've got no way to jail you or hold you prisoner, so your life expectancy at this point is what I say it is," John said.

"In other words, shut up," the man's handler whispered menacingly into his ear.

"Listen, I don't speak for all of us, but I know I was conscripted years ago. I love my country but I wanted to be a chemist, what you Americans call

THE WORLD BLEEDS

a pharmacist. I want nothing of these guns and death. I want to help people. What I don't want is my friends hurt or killed. It's all I have left of my homeland."

"I'll make you a deal," John said, pulling the rifle from the base of his skull and coming around to look the man in the eyes, "You help us with creating maps of where folks are stashed and other info and I will try to keep causalities to a minimum."

"You have what, eight men? You have no way to take the camp. You barely were able to take us," he said.

"Seven men, one woman. I can call up more as needed, but I think with your APC I have more than enough." John's voice was stern.

"Who are you?" one of the men on the ground asked.

"I'm just a simple country boy who grew up on a Ranch in Waxahachie Texas; that gal over there if I'm not mistaken was Miss Maryland about a decade or so back, John here is just a dirt farmer from this godforsaken state and the rest of these guys come from all walks of life. Who do you think we are?" Tex asked.

"The Devil," the trussed man on the end quipped.

"Close, but not quite The Devil. We're a lot worse."

The man spilled his guts completely. John was shocked at how few resources and men that they said were there. At first he thought it was a ruse to gain their confidence, but as they recounted the horrors of no supply lines, the illness of their own men, and not having the means or medicine to treat them, he began to believe differently. Eventually the rest of the men opened up as well. They relaxed a little when they realized they weren't going to be killed outright.

They helped the disabled men to their feet to approach the APC as one of the special ops team popped his head out of the hatch on top and gave them a thumbs up.

"Radio man never saw it coming. He's gagged," he called to them.

"Good. Somebody go collect your Lieutenant; we're going to set up camp somewhere."

"But… but he's dead?"

They waited in silence as Tex dragged Jenkins back into the open. His eyes were glazed in pain and a bloody streak ran down his shoulder above his bicep where a pressure bandage had been placed.

"Naw, I just gave his balls a little squeeze," Tex said showing the men one of his large callused hands, "And poked his shoulder a bit so you could see me wiping the blood off. Thing is, I think we are as sick of the killin' as the rest of folks are. So let's save some lives and I might let y'all live to see another day."

"You made him cry like that with a little squeeze of those hands?" Caitlin asked Tex, batting her eyelashes.

"Darlin', you ought to see what else I can do

THE WORLD BLEEDS

with these here hands. I'll have you know I'm the best masseuse in all of Alabama."

"That's because you're the only masseuse in Alabama," John grumbled, and a few of the rebels busted up laughing.

"Load 'em up boys," Caitlin urged and marched the captured solders in front of her and two others at gunpoint as the rest got into the APC.

CHAPTER 12

TALLADEGA FCI

Michael came to slowly. His head hurt, and every muscle in his body burned, like he'd just finished a strenuous workout. He opened his eyes to see he was lying on a rubber pad on a concrete floor. A stainless steel toilet was straight ahead and Michael rolled onto his back, the only direction that didn't require him to use his large muscle groups, which would cause more pain.

A single light bulb burned dimly behind a wire cage. The ceiling was speckled with water damage and the room had a musty smell overall. The walls were close together, perhaps an eight by eight squared off room with a steel door. A tray with a bottle of water sat on the shelf on the door, moisture still beading on the bottle. Michael sat up, suddenly more thirsty than in pain, and scooted closer to the tray.

A plate was covered with a napkin and two Aspirin were sitting in a plastic cup. Michael broke the seal on the water and considered the Aspirin, then upended the cup into his mouth and washed the pills down. With any luck, they would take the edge off the pain. He was pretty sure he'd been tasered again, but at a much higher level, and then clubbed into unconsciousness. He saw a small handwritten note under where the medicine cup had been, and was going to pick it up when his stomach protested loudly, and instead he lifted the napkin to see what he had for food.

Taking a swig from the bottle of water, he considered the sandwich. It was a plain bologna sandwich, a marvel of marvels. With the refrigeration gone, he realized that this had to have come from the Commander's food stores, as anything like that was long gone. Still, the Commander could have included some mayo or mustard…

Michael heard footsteps as he was finishing off the sandwich, the footfalls echoing. He gulped the last of the water with his back to the wall the door was on, and he heard a rattle of keys and a small slot opened.

"Put your dishes back on the tray and back away from the door," said someone, their legs the only thing that Michael could see in front of him.

Michael did so, but instead of backing up, he got closer to the slot and spoke, "Hey, where am I?"

he asked, reaching out to soldier on the other side.

A crackle of electricity was all he heard, half a heartbeat before what looked like the tip of a cattle prod sent jolts of electricity through his hand. Michael howled in pain, falling back into the cell. He curled there and screamed until he could get his body under control again. Red welts covered his wrist and top of his right hand and he held them in close to his body as he listened to footsteps walk away.

"Hey, you ok over there?" a familiar voice asked.

"Hurts, they tasered me again," Michael replied near the floor of the doorway where he figured he could get his voice out the best.

"Wait, Michael?" the voice asked incredulously. "Dad?"

§ § §

"Tonight's episode of Rebel Radio is going to focus on two topics that are probably problems for a lot of you nowadays. The kids will think it's funny, and many of you grown-ups are going to wrinkle your nose but hang in there, and Back Country J, our own Blake Jackson will be on in a moment to explain things to you. As it is, this is David," and he handed the mic over to his right, "And this is Patty," she said grinning before handing it back to David, "and hello world! Over."

The radio crackled as dozens of voices greeted David, Patty, Blake, and then each other. Since the

THE WORLD BLEEDS

mock up radio station began broadcasting regularly, new voices and people had started to reach out, helping each other. Sometimes they would run across small groups of people who needed help, sometimes military veterans or soldiers who were on vacation when the EMP happened. They shared information openly and freely on that channel, or at least the things they didn't want the NATO forces to know. It became like the president's fireside radio chat; a way for others around the country and world to follow along, and participate in helping a crippled nation and people.

"Good evening everyone. Couple of topics I want to talk to you all about: what to do when you have to go. Since the day we were born, we've never had a problem going to the bathroom, but I wanted to talk to you about disposal. I've listened on this frequency and we've had our Doc mention more than once that water pollution by waste is contributing to a lot of problems.

"When the power went off, it wasn't long until the toilets quit flushing. A ton of you probably found a spot and dug an outhouse. That works in the short term and, if you have enough land, it may not be a problem unless it contaminates your water supply. Some folks are using the restroom in lakes and rivers. If it worked in the pool and the water doesn't turn purple around you, you're safe right? Right?

"The problem is, we are all living in a closed loop now, and the few of us left are precious. I have a couple of ideas on what to do when you have to poo. Firstly, I'm no expert, I'm no doctor. I'm just a hillbilly who lives in the sticks with a great group of people. I can't even take credit for everything I'm about to share, because in the spirit of the purpose of this radio station, I learned something new and improved upon it. You should all do the same with the info you get here…" Blake paused to sip some water, "then share it with the rest of us."

"Now, I have an idea on how to take care of the waste, and it's been working on my homestead for a while now. We built a box. Nothing fancy, we just lined it with a big sheet of visqueen and stapled the edges on the outside of the box. It makes a great liner and it keeps the waste from contaminating things. Then you build a way to cover the front with glass. You can use old windows, storm doors, something you can open and close but keep a somewhat tight lid on. Poke or drill a small hole near the top of the box somewhere and staple some screen door screen over the hole and paint everything but the glass black.

"It works pretty simple. You do what you gotta do into a bucket, cover with sawdust, leaves or whatnot. When it's too full or fragrant, empty it into the bin. The heat will literally kill off any bacteria and essentially dry out the waste and the smell. It's a bigger version of a solar oven. When it gets too full, compost the dry stuff and use it for fertilizing your fruit trees, rose gardens and tulips. Any questions so far, over?"

THE WORLD BLEEDS

"Mr. Jackson, this is Z, you are saying build a big solar oven for poop, do I have that right, over?"

"Yes ma'am. But one that is pretty airtight, water tight and fly proof. I think more than forty percent of the illness we've heard about has been from drinking contaminated water. It's just one idea, and if folks have a better way, please share… Oh, and don't put the poo cooker by your house, for the same reasons you don't put the outhouse right against your bedroom window, over." Blake chuckled.

"Sounds good Mr. Jackson. What's the second thing you were going to share?"

"Drinking water. I almost forgot, thanks Z! There are a million ways to purify water. The easiest way is bleach; two drops per quart, eight drops per gallon of water. Cap it and let it sit for half an hour or so. Then open it up, pour it from one container to another until the smell of bleach dies down. If the water is terrible, use a little more, but don't overdo it. With iodine, it's five drops per quart, or twenty drops per gallon. If the water is too cloudy, with either method, you double it. Do not overdo it. Lastly, the method that has been used for thousands and thousands of years, boil the water. Let it cool, enjoy. This is important, since you don't know who's fouling the water upstream.

"Now, I'll be around for some questions and, if you know of a different or better way of doing things, don't hesitate to speak up. We're here to help each other and to get through the difficult times we're having. Over."

For thirty minutes, Blake and other survivors across the country shared information and news. The format of Rebel Radio hadn't changed much; share something big and then try to help individuals with their own particular situation. The topics were sometimes funny, sometimes serious. Tonight was a topic they ended up with a lot of bathroom euphemisms and jokes from everyone who had a microphone in their hands. Sandra sat in on that night's radio show like she often did and when her radio squawked on a different channel, she left the room for a moment and gave Blake a smile and a nod. She had info, but it could wait.

"If that's all we got for now, I'm going to leave you folks with David and Patty. I'll be back on tomorrow, same frequency, same time. Over and out," he said and then handed the mic over to David.

"Blake," Sandra said, leading him into the kitchen so they wouldn't interrupt David, "there are now four groups fixing to take on the FEMA camps. They're all small units like John's. They are going to attack the same time John does. There might be even more groups that we don't know about." Sandra told him.

"Coordinating the times... Hmmm... You think they are doing it so the other camps can't help each other out?" Blake asked his wife.

"Daddy, you're done!" Chris came out of nowhere and launched himself into the air.

Blake caught and spun him, feeling his shoulder

twinge in pain a little bit, but it was much better than it had been.

"What have you been doing buddy?" Blake said, putting him on the ground in front of a smiling Sandra.

"Playing with the rabbits. I got to help feed the chickens today too, and after school lessons I'll have some time to go picking some berries. Grandma Lisa says she's going to make us a PIE!" Chris's volume rose towards the end and he punctuated the last word with a fist pump.

Sandra snickered and Blake laughed.

"Where did you learn that?" Sandra asked, trying to get her composure back.

"I don't know. Something the kids in class do."

"Well," Blake said moving towards the doorway, "I guess that makes it ok for now. Come on, let's go see how the traps are doing on the back forty."

"Yes!"

"Got room on the quad for one more?" Sandra asked him, wrapping her arms around his neck.

"I've always got room for you, let's go… and Hon, do you think the coordination we were talking about earlier…?"

"Oh yeah, it's planned," he could see her grin as she came around in front of him and took his hand.

"Why do I have a feeling that you were in the middle of that somewhere?" Blake asked her, smiling back.

"That's cuz Mom gets into everything! Even lists!" Chris said and Blake busted up laughing as Sandra's face turned red and she sputtered for words.

"Let's go, I'll explain how to not stick your foot in your mouth someday."

§ § §

"The prisoners?" Caitlin asked, now fully dressed in black ACUs like the rest of the team.

"We're keeping the radioman, and the rest we're locking in an old barn," John told her.

"That means we have to come back and get them out," Tex said and a couple others nodded.

"Naw, I rigged up something. I tied the cuff keys to a piece of string. Other end I put inside a slice of a candle. When the candle burns down, the key drops into the guy's lap. Figure it'll give us about three or four hours," John told them.

There were blacked out faces, wearing watch caps that all nodded, they had used improvised timers like that before, whether a lit cigarette or a weighted two liter of pop as a counterweight with a small pinhole poked in the bottom.

"That'll give us enough time to do what we need to do." Caitlin said, and John nodded.

Henrikas had confirmed much of what the captured soldiers had said, and knowing morale was low and that many of the NATO soldiers were in America against their will, made John think it would be easy to try to keep his promise. If the small amount of soldiers were hit in the middle of

THE WORLD BLEEDS

the night, and the Commander taken, they could negotiate for the release of the prisoners without a terrific loss of life.

The biggest wildcard was the second APC. Without letting the radioman ask, which would have been suspicious, they had no idea if it was back at the camp, or out on patrol. They had a couple different ways to disable it, but it would help if it wasn't there for the main fight… the main gun was a horror if turned on people. Their plan was to disable or capture it outright. It was the biggest force multiplier they could get to take on the nearly 60 people working and guarding a camp of thousands.

CHAPTER 13

TALLADEGA FCI

"D ad? Is that you?" Michael asked in shock. "Yeah, it's me. What are you doing here?"

"We got back Stateside about a month after the EMP. They brought us here immediately. Have you seen your mother?" his tone was hopeful.

"No, no I haven't." Michael answered, worried.

"Did you find Grandpa's cave? Is that how you stayed out of Lukashenko's hands?"

"I've been in the camp for a little while now. I don't quite know where this is."

"We're in the second story of the hospital wing, psych unit. It's for trouble makers like me. I think the women and children are in a separate location," Michael's father said.

They spent the next two hours catching each

THE WORLD BLEEDS

other up. Michael's father had occupied the cell to the right of his ever since he had a public disagreement with Lukashenko. Michael also shared the bloodshed that had happened, his doubts of being a good man, and not having faith in his decisions. He then admitted to his father that he had killed Linny and Bret's father, and shared how he was too cowardly to admit it to the kids, even though he had taken them in as his own family.

"Son, I've never had to take a life before, and I can't say that I know how it feels, but Son... I'm proud of you."

"What?" Michael asked, lying on his stomach so he could get his head closer to the crack in the floor.

"I don't know if I could have done what you did, and I think what happened, well... You were put into an impossible situation and you came out OK. You handled it like a man. You shouldered the responsibility and Son... you make me proud."

Michael tried to swallow the lump in his throat, but failed. His mouth opened and closed to protest the words, and his body was fighting to sob or cry in relief. He absently rubbed his eyes to dislodge the dirt that had been making them leak a little bit, when shouts sounded at either end of the hallway and the sound of a heavy machine gun opening fire filled the air. Unlike the rifles the soldiers carried, this wasn't the loud whip crack. The sound was like some monstrous chainsaw wielded by a madman wearing a hockey mask, but even louder.

BOYD CRAVEN

"You promised not to kill them," the prisoner protested.

"We're only disabling the turret and chain gun. If they don't disengage, we will kill them." John told him grunting.

The interior of the APC was crowded, but already, four of the team had left an hour ago, once the APC had been let in through the first gate. Things hadn't gone well when the gate guards had requested to see Lieutenant Jenkins, so they just drove over the guard post, making him the first casualty of the war before he could get the alarm sounded. The revving of the twin motors drowned out the surprised yells.

"APC two on radio," Mouse, one of John's team said over his shoulder, not taking his eyes off the target.

"APC, we've disabled your primary guns. If you move your unit I will unload my rounds point blank into your unit. The armor you have cannot take a barrage like this for very long. I will have a team there in moments to remove you from the APC."

There was a long pause, and everyone inside John's APC was looking at the commotion stirring up as the sound of gunfire had awakened most everyone at camp. The raid had been timed for 3am, a time when most people would be asleep, or at their worst point of alertness.

"You will never make it out of here alive. I

suggest you back up and leave before you and your team are killed," the voice on the radio threatened.

John nodded to the prisoner who had pleaded for his friend's life and the microphone was handed to him.

"This is Saul, and these men are telling the truth. They do not care to kill you but I made a deal with them. Do not shoot at them and you will not be killed."

"Sounds too easy, doesn't it?" Tex asked no one in particular.

"Nothing's ever easy," Caitlin said, and then put her hand on Saul's shoulder, "tell him if they move that unit, we will be forced to kill them and the deal is off."

Saul grunted and repeated the message. In response, the enemy APC's engines roared and the APC moved to put its front in the way of the 12.7mm heavy machine gun.

"Lighting him up," Mouse said as the heavy gun began firing again.

An APC can move, but not as fast as a speeding bullet, and the second the tires and sides of the unit got pounded, the armor on the old unit failed in a spot. Smoke billowed out of the hatches and screams filled the radio, begging them to stop.

"Unit neutralized." Mouse's voice was soft, in contrast to the ex-biker's appearance.

"Ok, moving." John told them, opening the hatch, helping first Tex and then Caitlin out, as the rest of the team remained in the APC.

"Light up those guard towers. Cut them down, and if they start firing rockets, put the rounds into the men. I made a promise, but I don't expect to keep it if it means losing American lives."

"You got it boss," Mouse shouted over the din of the motors and the cycling of the gun.

"Hon, you ready to move it, or are we going to get a table for three?" Caitlin asked.

"Yeah, let's get out of here before the guards…" John's voice was cut off as troops came running towards them, three abreast, firing carbines at them.

They rolled behind the APC for cover and aimed between the big tires, wincing every time a ricochet got close.

"Ut oh." Tex grumbled, a finger pointing up.

John looked up and saw the heavy gun moving towards the advancing troops. He expected them to break for cover, but they kept converging, spraying bullets until they had to reload mags. When the gun opened up, it was slightly louder than a locomotive making love to a 747, and the bullets shredded flesh in an explosion of gore.

"That was ugly. They must have thought the burning APC was us," John said with a sick look in his eyes.

"Let's go, we're too far out in the open," Tex said, checking his gear before standing up.

§ § §

Michael couldn't hear his father anymore; the

shouting of the prisoners and the gunfire from outside was too much. Short bursts of gunfire would be answered by long strings of it, and a lot of cursing. Three simultaneous explosions made it feel like the oxygen was sucked out of the room, but Michael instinctively knew that if they had gone off inside the building where they were being held, they would be dead from the concussion alone.

Through all of that, and the rising smell of smoke, he could hear the door at the end of the hallway being kicked open. Those in the isolation cells fell silent and he could hear keys jingling. Pleas, then screams and gunfire abruptly ended the begging. The keys jingled again, shocked screams and gunfire. The keys jingled closer, the cycle repeated.

"Dad, Dad, they're shooting us." Michael said.

"Son, I want you to know I love you. I always will. Both your mother and I have always been proud of you." Michael winced as a door closer was kicked by an inmate.

Keys, screams, gunfire. The isolation unit screamed as a whole, as the realization hit everyone and Michael stood, uncertain what to do. He could hear the keys to his right now, and his father's screams. A new sound overrode that. The sound of mortal agony and then two short gunshots ended the sound. Almost in a panic, Michael moved to the right side of the door, where the hinges were. He could tell the door opened inwards and, if he was lucky, he could make it hard for them before he died.

The keys jangled just outside the door and, as it opened, it was kicked back hard. Michael cringed, but pressed himself into the wall as much as he could, the heavy steel door almost slamming his head through the wall. He held his breath.

"He's in here somewhere, you take care of him, I'm going to get the rest." A deep voice said, but Michael couldn't recognize it over the screams coming from nearby.

Sweat trickled down his face, running into his eyes making them sting. He waited, even as his brain was begging for him to breathe, to act, to flee. A barrel of a carbine slowly poked in front of the door, where Michael could see, and he pushed the steel door and latched on the end of the barrel, pushing it away. Gunfire strafed the ceiling and he pulled at the carbine's barrel and strap with all of his strength until he felt the gun pop free from the owner's grip. In a panic, he over compensated it and it went flying across the room, skittering into a corner.

Michael's vision narrowed and he leapt for the gun, landing on his hands and knees, scrabbling, expecting blows to rain down on his head, back, legs. Maybe the taser, they loved using a taser, especially on him.

"I won't…" Tears threatened to blind him as he started to exact revenge for the death of his—

"Dad?" Michael shouted, lowering the gun and running to his father, crushing him in an embrace.

THE WORLD BLEEDS

"But how?"

"Big guy, tall, black. Looked like he could…" Michael's dad stopped and looked to where Michael was staring.

"We have to move if we're going to get your kids out," King said, his voice rumbling.

King was in poor shape and bleeding in several places. What looked like a long furrow was cut through the skin of his left shoulder and he was dropping blood off his chin from a cut under his eye. Besides the ring of keys, he held a pistol.

"Do you know where they are?" Michael asked him hopefully, trying to hand the carbine to his father.

"I do, and you better keep that." Michael's father said, pushing the gun back into his arms.

An explosion made the floor shake and King looked at them, as the rest of the prisoners from that level ran for the staircase at the far end of the doorway.

"We really have to go," King told the Lewiston men.

§ § §

John had split off from the group. His next target was right in front of him, a young soldier who, despite the chaos, was carefully guarding the door to the women's dorms. Using the shadows and watching the young NATO soldier, he moved as close as he could when he kicked an empty shell casing, causing it to skitter across the pavement and draw the attention of the man. The barrel of the man's gun rose, but with regret, John stitched the man with the M2, now running full out because his element of surprise was lost.

As the guard slid to the ground leaving a red smear on the doorway, John was picking up the fallen gun, putting the M2's sling across his shoulders. He checked to make sure there wasn't another guard on the other side of the door before easing inside.

Immediately the smell of unwashed bodies and filth almost overwhelmed him. Rows of keys lined the walls and John grabbed some meant for the first row. Not seeing anyone down the long narrow hallway that ran through the whole facility, he fumbled with the lock. When the lock clicked open, John slammed the door back in a hurry, covering the room in case somebody was lying in wait. The room was empty except for a ragged woman in filthy stained white pants and a cotton tank top. It was immediately obvious she hadn't had a shower or wash in quite some time, yet she cowered in the corner terrified.

"Ma'am. I'm here to get you out of here. Do you need help walking?" John asked, hoping, dreaming, wishing she could, because they didn't have enough manpower to carry out a lot of wounded.

"You… you're American?" she asked in a hoarse whisper, not meeting his gaze.

"Yes ma'am. We're here to bust everyone out."

THE WORLD BLEEDS

"Took you long enough." The woman wiped her face with her forearm and stood up and gave John a long appraising look.

It took her a few seconds to get the courage to lift her eyes to meet his gaze, but when she did, she saw the sincerity in his features. She immediately relaxed inside and straightened her posture. She was nearly as tall as John, but she'd missed a lot of meals and her skin hung loose from her frame. Still, there was something about her that John recognized. Despite her act moments ago, this woman had a backbone of steel and she had been biding her time.

"Can you help me get everyone else out of here?" John asked, and had to raise his voice at the end as the big 12.7mm machine gun of the APC opened up again.

"Yes, I just need a set of keys. There's a master key on each ring."

John tossed her a set and then went from cell to cell. He didn't waste time in explaining anything, but just started opening doors. Slowly, by twos and threes, women and young ladies left the cells and stood dumbfounded in the hallway, too scared to move without instruction.

"Shake your asses ladies, we're getting out of here!" The first woman that John freed had yelled over the growing din of voices.

The smell was rising and John had more places to be, so he made sure he was the first one out of the door and he saw part of his team firing sporadically, towards the guard towers. Tex and Caitlin must have gotten the men's dorms freed, because as soon as the ladies saw the men, they surged past John, almost running. Husbands and wives met in fierce embraces. Daughters yelled for their fathers, and a flood of short people came boiling out of the building to the west of the woman's dorms. Kids!

CHAPTER 14

Commander Lukashenko already had his go pack ready and on his back. He'd armed himself from his personal kit; what he'd always thought of as his get-out-alive pack. He knew his orders were a joke, he knew what he was doing was wrong, but he was a soldier, a career soldier. It was laughable that sixty men were assigned to manage a camp of many, many thousands of people. When the facility had been a fully functioning federal prison, a normal staff consisted of hundreds of personnel. It had always made him nervous to be so outnumbered.

He was a soldier, not a prison warden!

His efforts of bringing Michael into the fold of most day to day operations had been sincere, because he wanted the others to realize that he was stuck just as bad as they were… but he knew the big plan, the big picture and, as much as he loathed his orders, he felt they were necessary if America was to survive. Now, Michael had spit in his face, and having him moved into isolation seemed like it should have been done after the first incident. He'd tried, he'd tried to show the inmates his merciful side, but even the kind Michael had turned on him… It had been a disaster and even his men were whispering behind his back, wondering if he was fit for command. "*I should have just had the boy killed*," he thought to himself bitterly.

Without America, the world would be a very scary place as the voice of ISIS would spread like wildfire across the globe. Convert or die. England and Greece were the first to succumb to civil war after America's fall, while Lukashenko's own men were being shipped stateside. Heavy bombing and eventually glassing Iran and Saudi Arabia with high yield nuclear bombs was the only thing that made the Jihadists pause long enough for the EU to regroup and fight back. If only he could have gotten a pause here in this facility, he may not be running for his life with a pistol style AK, an original AK with a dozen mags and half a tin of ammo in his pack. Every move he made sounded like wind chimes, he clinked so much.

He knew he was dangerously overloaded, but judging by the sounds, explosions and the destruction, an army of at least battalion strength was attacking. It never occurred to him that such a

THE WORLD BLEEDS

small team, well equipped with intelligence, could do so much damage. Never the less, he was bugging out before the inmates turned angry and tore him limb from limb.

As Lukashenko ghosted out of the now darkened offices and into the smoky moonlight, trying to make his way past the high security lockup, the doors burst open and the prisoners emptied out, following the large crowd heading towards the open front gate. He almost paused to shout, but everywhere he looked, he saw dead or disabled men from his unit and, if the inmates, workers, prisoners – whatever they should be called - were all loose, they'd tear him and his men to pieces. If he had any men left.

He was backing into the shadows when he saw a large block of a man, as dark as night, exit the building right in front of him. King. He was followed by a tall but gaunt white man, one he recognized as being one of the boat people that the National Guard had dropped off in the beginning. He was a man who loved to quote scripture aloud and spread dissention with the population at large. The Commander himself had given the order to put him in the isolation units of the old hospital ward converted into solitary. When the third figure emerged, it was all he could do not to empty his gun into the man-child. Michael.

§ § §

129

John was working against the flow of bodies. Any of the NATO forces who had surrendered were escorted to a holding cell. Some of them had looked relieved, which puzzled John when he first happened across it, but he was letting Caitlin and Tex keep track of them as he went building to building, making sure everyone who wanted to leave could. Some folks were too scared to move at first, and he left them, figuring they would come out on their own as they planned to leave the gates open afterwards.

Out of the corner of his eye, John saw Michael's father and Michael exit a building just behind a large black man who was covered in blood, carrying a pistol. John almost called out, in surprise and joy to see his neighbor alive and safe. If Michael had found him, had they found Linny and Bret? He moved through the crowd of panicked people towards two of his own, trying to scan for threats.

"John?" Michael shouted pointing so his father could follow his line of sight.

"Michael, have you seen the kids?" John screamed back, scores of people separating them as they fled the compound.

"No, not since they separated us when we first got here." Michael called back.

The sound of the heavy machine gun opening up again was deafening. They must have reloaded and now one of the remaining guard towers was being turned into small wooden toothpicks by the relentless fire. Everyone winced when an explosion rocked the disintegrating building, but the crowd kept moving.

§ § §

Lukashenko had found a good spot to follow Michael unobserved, and was shocked to his roots when a man in black combat dress stepped out to the crowd and called for him. Their familiarity had almost sent him into a fit of rage, but then he looked closer at the gaunt man by Michael's side. The family resemblance was unmistakable. Both of them were trouble makers and now one of the men attacking his command was speaking with…

Lukashenko didn't believe in coincidences and he now had three people literally within his sights who had brought ruin upon him, and potentially stranded him in a foreign land. His hands barely shook as he raised the AK pistol, using both hands to steady things.

§ § §

Michael's father saw something out of the chaos, burning buildings, press of bodies fleeing and screams. A gun barrel broke into the moonlight from the deep shadows, and the Commander stepped into the moonlight. His face was a rictus of anger, pain and hate. The barrel swung in their direction over the crowd of running people as the Commander stepped up on a stone planter. With horror, he realized that Michael was right in the line of fire. He tried to scream, but there was too much noise and, as he tried to push his son down and out of the way, bullets tore through his malnourished body instead.

He only felt the first two impacts as pain. Falling, he saw his son's shocked expression. Pistol fire was louder than the immediate crowd, and a dark blur launched itself towards the Commander's location. King. All strength seemed to flow out of him. Too weak to move, every breath labored, Michael took his hand and pulled himself close to his father.

"Proud of you son," was the last thing he whispered to Michael, before falling back. He closed his eyes for one last, long sleep.

§ § §

THE HOMESTEAD KENTUCKY

"Baby, you remember the young man that was with John, down in Alabama?" Sandra asked.

"Yeah, wasn't he one of the ones in the camps? I'm still waiting on hearing news on the progress" Blake asked as Chris crawled up on his lap near the radio.

"Yes, that's him. We've been getting updates on the scrambled channel," Sandra said, sitting down and ruffling her son's hair, "Alabama's camps have minimal loss of life, most of it being the NATO forces who didn't surrender. Michael and the kids he was taking care of made it out fine."

"Something's bothering you. I can tell," Blake told his wife.

"In the escape, Michael's father was killed. There is no sign of his mother, and the Commander of the facility got away."

"Oh, no." Blake stood to stretch.

Patty, who had given up her seat, slid back in and switched to the scrambled frequency and soon updates were pouring in from the southern parts of the country. They all listened for a while before Blake took Chris by the hand and pulled him into the kitchen. The news was good, but not good enough that he wanted to depress his son with it.

"Daddy, what are we doing in here?" Chris asked Blake, who was pulling some supplies out of the cupboard.

"There's a kid in Alabama who lost his parents tonight, buddy. I don't know if you remember what that's like, before mom and I… but I think there's something we can do together. That boy loved to go cat fishing, so let's make us some stink bait and dough balls and try our luck with a bunch of the kids in the next few days."

"The kids? Really? Will Momma let you go without her?"

"Who says I'm not going? You think a girl can't go fishing?" Her tone was stern but her eyes twinkled and a smile tugged at the corners of her mouth.

"No ma'am. I just thought you'd be busy." Chris answered, sounding solemn.

"I think the thing that hit home the hardest for me tonight," Sandra said, "is that there's never enough time with family and friends."

Blake nodded and pulled Chris into a noogie and rubbed his noggin for a minute before getting the flour out with a measuring cup.

"First, we have to make some dough balls, and maybe in the end, we'll bake the hooks inside of them so they stay on longer. Then we have to find something stinky to coat them with. It could be chicken guts, some liver, or some—"

"We could use some of mom's cooking!" Chris said, despite the giggles, and flew out of the doorway before a sputtering Sandra took chase.

Lisa walked upstairs to see what the running was about and gave Blake a puzzled look.

"No worries Mom, just horsing around." Blake told his mother in law.

"Do I need to take a switch to you?" she asked, grinning.

"No, but your grandson might not get some of your home made brownies if Sandra catches him first." He chuckled.

"She didn't do too well with my recipe yesterday. She'll get better, don't you and Chris worry about starving," Lisa patted Blake on the shoulder and walked outside into the starlight, letting the sounds of a chase and the combined voices of laughter filter into the house.

THE WORLD BLEEDS

To be notified of new releases, please sign up for my mailing list at: http://eepurl.com/bghQb1

Book 6 is out! Get your copy here: http://www. amazon.com/gp/product/B0164N9LE2

A side story that takes place concurrently with this one, with a lot of the same characters you meet here, is available now. It's novel length, so I hope you enjoy! Here's *Rebel Radio*: http://www.amazon. com/dp/B013L2F5GC

Good Fences is a novel in the same world as *The World Burns*, and *Good Fences* has character interaction via radio with the Homestead! Pick up your copy here: http://www.amazon.com/ Good-Fences-Scorched-Earth-Novel-ebook/dp/ B015WUE1NY

ABOUT THE AUTHOR

Boyd Craven III was born and raised in Michigan, an avid outdoorsman who's always loved to read and write from a young age. When he isn't working outside on the farm, or chasing a household of kids, he's sitting in his Lazy Boy, typing away.

http://www.boydcraven.com/
Facebook: https://www.facebook.com/boydcraven3
Email: boyd3@live.com
You can find the rest of Boyd's books on Amazon:
http://www.amazon.com/-/e/B00BANIQLG

33311020R20089

Made in the USA
San Bernardino, CA
29 April 2016